Beneath the Surface

*A Journal of Life & Love During
the Great Copper Strike of 1913*

THEY FOUGHT TO LIVE. HE LIVED TO FIGHT.

J.P. HALL

July 23, 1913
Miners vote to strike.

July 27, 1913
Waddell-Mahon Corporation guards arrive from New York.

July 30,1913
Michigan Militia arrive to C & H strike zone.

August 14, 1913
Seeberville murders. Alois Tijan & Steve Putrich died from "waddie" gunfire at a Seeberville boardinghouse.

August 10-24, 1913
Champions of American Labor arrive to the zone in support of the miners. The likes of John Mitchell (United Mine Workers of America) and Mother Jones added publicity to the strike.

September 20, 1913
Judge O'Brien grants a temporary order against striker demonstrations.

September 29, 1913
Judge O'Brien rules that C & H failed to provide sufficient evidence against the miners. He revokes the earlier order.

October 1, 1913
Judge O'Brien rejects C & H appeal to his reversal. C & H takes their case to the Michigan Supreme Court.

October 8, 1913
Michigan Supreme Court upholds the 9/20 ruling.

October 10, 1913
Trainloads of strikebreakers arrive from Ascher Detective Agency. Trains are continually attacked by striking miners.

November 10, 1913
The press announces the existence of the Citizens' Alliance, a group joined to stop the WFM from spreading "poisonous propaganda".

November 27, 1913
Truth, the Citizens' Alliance mouthpiece begins publication.

December 5, 1913
Judge O'Brien suspends sentences for 139 he had previously found guilty of contempt of court for violating the earlier injunction.

December 7, 1913
Painesdale murders. Three scabs killed by assumed WFM assailants. WFM blames the strikebreaker thugs.

December 8-12, 1913
C &H shuts off water and electric at company homes. Citizens' Alliance members raid WFM headquarters and members' homes for weapons and ammunition.

December 16, 1913
The Supreme Court issues a permanent injunction against the strikers prohibiting all demonstrations.

December 24, 1913
The WFM's lawyer had previously petitioned Judge O'Brien for an injunction against the Citizens' Alliance Members for violence against the strikers. Finally, on this day, he rules against the Alliance members. Italian Hall Tragedy. 3 Italians, 20 Croations or Slovenians, and 50 Finnish perish. Sixty of the victims were between the ages of 2 and 16.

April 12, 1914
Four locals vote to end the strike. The Calumet local was the only local that voted to continue the strike.

LAKE

RED
CAL
OSC
BOSTON
HUBBE
REDRIDGE
HANCO
FREDA

HOUGHTON
HURONTOWN
ATLANTIC
SOUTH RANGE
TRIMOUNTAIN   BALTIC
PAINESDALE
SEEBERVIL

HOUGHTON   CO.

BARAGA

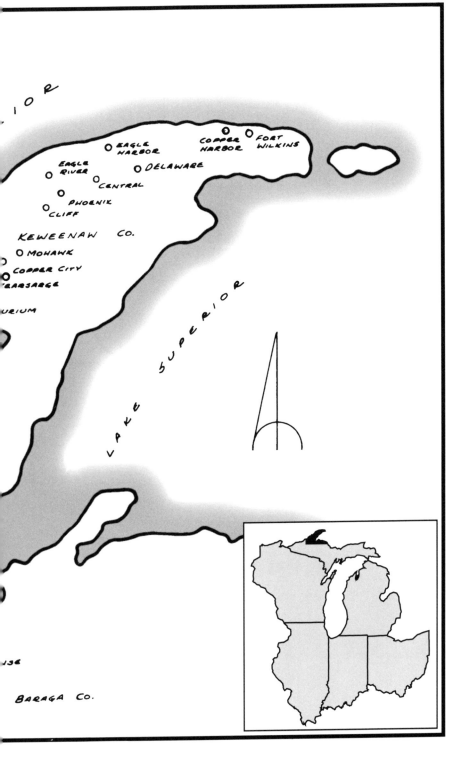

© 2001 J.P. Hall

ISBN 0-9712148-0-8
Library of Congress Control Number 2001092216
Published by P.I.A., Inc., Petticoat Press
Marquette, Michigan 49855

Printed in the United States of America by
Lake Superior Press
Marquette, Michigan 49855

First Edition 2001

Photos provided by:
Jack Deo of Superior View in Marquette, Michigan.
Michigan Technological University Archives
and Copper Country Historical Collections
in Houghton, Michigan.

This book is dedicated to those
who died or had their lives tarnished
by the Great Copper Strike of 1913.

December 24, 1959

Eston watches the last minute Christmas shoppers from his brownstone window. The light snow falling, just in time for the holiday, seems to have put a gait in their steps. The only sound in his mahogany paneled study is the persistent tick of his mantel clock. Stacks of folders, awaiting entries, occupy every spare inch of space. Eston moves to the fireplace mantel, where he has placed the only semblance of Christmas in his study. His liver spotted hands finger the tattered pink crepe tree ornament. As he moves to his desk, the phone rings. Eston hesitates to answer, as he is lost in memories of a time long ago, one with memories so powerful that they'll forever be etched in his mind and burn to his soul.

What a beautiful day in Red Jacket! What a beautiful day to turn 20 years old! By far, today is the best weather I've seen since our arrival in March. Father didn't give me the facts about Upper Michigan winters when convincing Mother and me to make the move from Boston, so that he could take the position as mine captain at Calumet & Hecla Mining Company. He said simply, "Winters are longer and you'll see more snowfall." He was right about that fact. The ice didn't leave the harbor until mid-April, and a few of the 200 inches of snow that we had received still lay on the ground in May. Today, however, things are greatly improved. The thermometer reads close to 70 degrees. The slight breeze through my open window is a condition that I thought I'd never so treasure. The weather certainly is making it difficult to focus on the many accounting journals stacked around me. Being an accountant is so dreary. I can't wait to get back to Boston to further my education in writing. I haven't broken the news to Father that I want to be a playwright. At least I can live vicariously through the visiting players of Red Jacket's opera house until I can return to the university. Mother has planned a birthday dinner with Sheriff Cruse's family. Apparently the sheriff and Father need to discuss the tensions arising between the copper miners' union and C & H. This is about as exciting as things get here in the Keweenaw!

The birthday dinner was interesting. It was more like a strikebreaker party. Father and the sheriff talked incessantly about the Western Federation of Miners' Union and their demands. As usual, the workers want more pay and shorter workdays. Also, they want to go back to using the two-man drill. They claim that the new one-man drill, which they've nicknamed "the widow maker", is dangerous and only benefits the owners at the expense of the miners' safety. They may be onto something. This morning Solomon, the mine's oldest worker, was killed by falling rock while operating the one-man drill. It was probably time for him to retire anyway. Mother tried to play matchmaker with Romaine, the sheriff's daughter and me. She's definitely not my preference, but fun to tease. We went for a walk after dinner down Fifth Street. What a hodgepodge of immigrants! We never heard English spoken the whole time we strolled. You name it…Italian, Finnish, Polish, German…we heard it! Romaine's clutch on my arm never loosened. Out of prudence, we didn't linger and I escorted her home earlier than planned.

July 3, 1913

Father's at it again. He wants me to be the scapegoat at the Fourth of July C & H picnic. Father knows that he'll run into Charles Moyer, the President of the Western Federation of Miners' Union. Moyer wants the C & H owners to recognize the union. He's doing all that he can to pressure the mine owners. In fact, Father came across a flyer, with his name on it, posted on a street lamp that read JAMES HARLOW MUST GO! He was pretty unnerved. "Eston, my son, I want you to represent C & H at the corporate picnic. I want you to find out what the miners are planning. I don't know how many more displays of discontent can be accepted without ramifications. The workers don't realize just how good they have it here in the Keweenaw. They've got free water and electricity. The rent for a company house is only six dollars a month. Maybe you can remind them of what they're taking for granted." I knew better than to argue with Father. In accepting to represent the corporation at the picnic, I also negotiated a larger allowance so that I could attend the upcoming play Saturday night at the opera house. Father calls it "drivel".

~ *Fifth Street, Calumet**. ~

* Red Jacket officially became Calumet in 1929. The village fathers explained that "frequently people come to Red Jacket looking for Calumet, and others are in Red Jacket, believing they are in Calumet and cannot find their way to Red Jacket. To add to the confusion the Calumet postoffice is situated in Red Jacket. The name Calumet applies to the entire community, with the exception of Laurium." Application was made to the state legislature, approval came, and on June 3, 1929 by a village vote of 172 to 7 the town name of Red Jacket was relegated to history.

I think that all of the 30,000 residents of Red Jacket, Calumet and Laurium were on C & H armory grounds today. It was sweltering hot, but that didn't seem to stop the miners and their families from celebrating our nation's birthday. Aside from one small group of miners, which included Charles Moyer, everyone seemed to be enjoying the C & H sponsored picnic. It was fun to watch the different groups of immigrants eventually separate into their own sections of yard. Much like their neighborhoods are separated, so are their picnics. A small fight broke out among some "Cousin Jacks", Cornish miners; and some "Micks", Irish miners. Their feuds never seem to cease. Fortunately one of the Irish wives doused the rumbling men with a big bucket of cold water. It was quite the humorous sight. Among the crowd, I spotted the most beautiful teacher's aide. I watched her serve watermelon to the children. Her blonde hair floated around her head like a halo. When I approached her and introduced myself as Eston, son of James Harlow, she turned right on her heel and walked away. I'm sure she's charmed.

I'm not sure why Saturdays are spent working on our new $85,000 house. It would seem that nothing could be in need of attention at that price. Nonetheless, Mother had Father and me supervising the plantings near the front porch. As we worked, we discussed the group of miners that demonstrated at the beginning of the Fourth of July parade. The women carried signs that read DON'T LET THE ONE-MAN DRILL KILL and ONE-MAN MACHINE–OUR WIDOW MAKER. Big Annie, the President of the WFM's Women's Auxiliary, led the way waving a twelve foot flag. We're simply amazed at the conviction of some of the women. As we were laughing about Big Annie, Sheriff Cruse pulled up to the house to tell us that another worker, aged 30, had his neck broken by a falling boulder. He left a widow and six children.

After Sheriff Cruse's visit on Saturday, Father's mood grew very dark. He quit working on the yard and retired to his study. His cursory mood had Mother in tears by dinner. I could not escape to the opera house quickly enough. Feeling rebellious, I took in some spirits at McGrath's pub. Clara, the flamboyant barkeep, recognized me from the Fourth of July picnic. She was friendly to me even though she knew I was against WFM demands. It isn't that I'm for or against. I'm just indifferent. I'd rather not be involved in the mine's operations at all. Getting out of the Keweenaw is my main priority. Clara and I discussed my aspirations to be a playwright. She too has interests in the theater. Perhaps that's why she tolerated me in her pub. Many believe that Clara's reputation is questionable and that she may run a house of ill repute. Her boardinghouse is called the Hennery because of the number of unmarried women who lodge there. She claims that many are young girls studying to be teachers. Nobody believes her story. As I was talking with Clara, the beautiful blond from the picnic ran in, whispered something to her and then ran out of the saloon. I was tongue-tied as I asked Clara about the beautiful girl. I found out that her name is Aili Maki and that she lives with Clara at the boardinghouse. The play was a blur. Aili consumed my thoughts.

A miner operating the "widow maker" or one-man drill.

5

Monday brought me out of my fog, largely because Father's bad mood from Saturday carried over to the new week. Once again he was shocked by the defiance of the miners' wives. This time, dressed in their Sunday best, from 6 a.m. until 11 a.m., they paraded the streets of Red Jacket. What really angered him was that they greeted the miners at the mine entrance, company property, as they clocked in for work. Again, their signs called for the end of the one-man drill and for better disability and survivor benefits. "Christ!" said Father. "What will they want next? We have to put a stop to this nonsense before the wives and striking miners gain more support." He wants me to audit the medical records at the C & H Memorial Hospital to find out just how many injuries or deaths there have actually been. "I'll show them that their justifications are wrong," Father stammered. My appointment with Blanche Whitford, the head nurse, is scheduled for Wednesday.

After dinner last night, I went back to McGrath's for a nightcap. It was a beautiful night. The air here does seem more pure than in Boston. Calumet, does have some redeeming qualities considering its remote locale. Due to the huge profits of the mining companies, the villages have more in regard to amenities than some larger cities. Paved roads, electric street lamps and cable cars arrived here way before other larger communities. Walking down Fifth Street's boarded sidewalk, I was reminded of Boston's main avenue. Clara was working again, and as usual, she greeted me with a smile. Nonchalantly, or so I thought, I asked her a few questions about Aili. In answering my questions, I found out that Aili has been an orphan since her mother's death during her birth, that she's a teacher's aide and that if I touch her I'm a dead man. Apparently, my intentions were all too clear. "Besides," said Clara, "she'd have nothing to do with you because of your position at the mine." This explains why she abruptly walked away from me at the picnic. Father surely wouldn't be pleased with the relationship anyway, as she's not educated or wealthy. Nonetheless, I'm interested.

Today Father met for hours with Sheriff Cruse. He wants the sheriff to patrol the mine entrances at the start and end of each shift. He wants him to ask Judge Murphy if there is anything legal that can be done to stop the demonstrations on mine property, which oddly enough really encompasses all but a few plots of Red Jacket, Laurium and Calumet. The sheriff said that he'd look into the situation further. I met with Blanche at the hospital the first thing this morning. Her daughter Marian is one of the few women in Red Jacket that I've courted. Marian's father and mother moved here from Boston too, so we have a lot to grumble about together. She has plans to attend college in Boston, but like my life, hers too was put on hold so that her father could pursue profits as part owner of the mine. She is delicate enough, but seems to have a sharp tongue at times. Marian also works at the hospital alongside her mother. As I greeted them this morning at the nurse's desk, I saw Aili out of the corner of my eye. Dressed in volunteer whites, she was pushing a patient towards me in a wheelchair. Our eyes met, but before I could act, she turned down an adjacent corridor.

∼ Sheriff Cruse on a good day! ∼

The numbers that I presented him after my audit of the patient files did not please Father. Since the one-man drill was introduced, the hospital has averaged two maiming injuries and one death each week. Father can no longer argue against the miners' concerns for safety or lack of disability insurance. Issues aside, he is still unwilling to yield to their demands. "If they don't like it, they can leave!" he ranted. "New immigrants arrive daily, so we have a ready supply of workers. With the price of copper dropping daily, we can't afford to go back to the two-man drill." Profit is the name of the game. After I met with Blanche yesterday, I had lunch with Marian in the canteen. She was very flirtatious and coerced me into taking her down to Fifth Street to hear the Red Jacket Municipal Band perform at their biweekly street performance. The festivities are offered by the shop owners to promote more downtown shopping. While we enjoyed our ice milk and watched the performance, I spotted Aili among the crowd. I excused myself from Marian for a moment and went in search of Aili. As Aili noticed my approach, she tried to quickly walk in the other direction. I grabbed her elbow and turned her around so that she had to face me. The music seemed to disappear as she spoke her first words to me: "Eston Harlow, kindly let go of my elbow." We both smiled at her rhyme and stood facing each other for what seemed to be an eternity. I could not help but lose myself in her crystal blue eyes. I badly wanted to touch her blond curls, her dimpled chin and porcelain skin. She too seemed to devour my appearance. My voice shook as I asked her to accompany me to the shore on Saturday. She hesitated but eventually I heard her words of agreement. Nervous, she quickly melted back into the crowd, but not without one more glance in my direction. Marian was not amused when I returned. Luckily she hadn't seen me conversing with Aili. I could not wait to escort Marian home. Her sour mood turned flirtatious during the walk home. I think that my disinterest is driving Marian mad.

Most of today was spent compiling production reports. With the price of copper falling due to increased competition, Father and some other regional mine owners have banded together to try to fix the price of copper on the market by decreasing or increasing production depending on the situation. This is helpful, but not the answer to declining profits. In 1890, C & H produced nearly 60 percent of Michigan's copper. Today it's closer to 40 percent and dropping. The owners have their work cut out for them. I passed by McGrath's on my way home to ask a favor of Clara. Knowing that she must be aware of my afternoon plans with Aili, I felt safer asking her instead of Mother to prepare a picnic basket for our day at the shore. She gave me a raised eyebrow to let me know that she wasn't pleased that I was pursuing Aili. "She's too good for you, my friend. She's got a heart of gold. The only reason I'm willing to help is because Aili seems to be equally enamored with you." With a grin she said, "The basket will be ready by the time the train leaves. Now get out of here."

Another letter from the striking miners arrived at the office today. I brought the unopened letter into Father's office. With one look at the WFM return address, he pulled out his return-to-sender stamp, stamped the letter and threw it back into the outgoing mail bin. "It will be a cold day in hell before I'll meet with Mr. Moyer," he told me. "Besides, I know that in event of a strike, the WFM doesn't have the funds to support 9,000 miners and their families for very long." All the while we were discussing Moyer, the rebellious miners, now reaching numbers close to 100, were outside marching the streets of Red Jacket. Father and I looked out the office window to watch the spectacle. Not far behind Big Annie's pace was Aili. She too was waving the American flag in support for the miners' rights. Dear God! What will Father think if he finds out that I'm smitten with one of the strikers?

I told Mother and Father that I was going to work today to finish some audits. They seemed to buy my story. I picked Aili up at Clara's boarding-house on Mine Street by mid-morning. Clara greeted me with a smile and a basket full of nourishment. Aili looked angelic as she came down the steps. She had her hair done up in a twist and looked much older than her seventeen years. As she grabbed her parasol and wrap, she finally looked my way. Her face turned crimson as she said, "Good Morning. Shall we go?" She pecked Clara on the cheek, and we were off. We caught the Keweenaw Central Railroad train to Crest View just as it was leaving the station. Once seated, we found that we were at a loss for words. Finally I said, "Did you enjoy your march yesterday?" With that she had to laugh and the ice was broken. Aili cares deeply about the miners' cause. She told me about the deaths and injuries that she has seen at the hospital. She also sees firsthand the devastation that arises when a miner dies. She sees fatherless children every day. Often it seems that they're orphaned because the mothers have to work long hours just to put food on the table. Many of the children also work long hours. Her passion for others made me feel like a shallow rogue. Perhaps profits aren't everything. We exited the train in Crest View and had horses waiting to take us the rest of the way to the Eagle River beach pavilion. The weather was perfect as we picnicked and searched for agates along the beach. I found a beautiful agate for Aili to keep. She was flattered by my small token and vowed never to remove it from her pocket.

⁓ Daily, this is what I see from my office window.
Aili, of course, is usually front and center. ⁓

I can't believe how smart and talented Aili is considering her upbringing. Not only does she work as a teacher and hospital volunteer, but also she works at the Red Jacket Opera House as a stage hand and wardrobe assistant. Father was called to the mine to break up a fight among some strikers and non-strikers. Sheriff Cruse and some of his deputies also arrived at the mine and helped to disperse the growing crowd. Several arrests were made for violations of conduct and trespassing. After helping Mother around the house, I walked to Section Sixteen Park. The wooded recreation area was crowded, but I found a quiet spot to spread a blanket. Before I could get lost in my thoughts of Aili, Marian and her half-wit brother, James, asked if they could join me. Reluctantly, I answered in the affirmative. After an afternoon of uneasy relaxation, the three of us walked home. As we passed the Red Jacket Cemetery, we saw Aili placing flowers on her mother's grave. As we passed, Marian greeted her and grabbed my elbow. Aili nodded to Marian, looked me in the eyes and then turned away to tend to her mother's grave.

Today was unbearable at work. Father and the owners were at odds all day about how to handle the strike situation. Governor Ferris summoned Judge Alfred Murphy, Wayne County Circuit Court Judge, to come to the meeting so that they could discuss their rights as property owners. The judge basically said that at this point, the strikers haven't done anything wrong by merely demonstrating. There was nothing that he could do, but he did agree to telegram the state governor to see how similar strikes across the country are being handled. After work, I walked downtown to the *Mining Gazette* to place an ad for the vacant mine positions. Clara ran into me as she exited the City Drug Store. She let me have it! Aili told her that she had seen me courting Marian. She told me to stay away from her, especially since Marian and Aili sometimes work together at the hospital. I tried to tell her that Marian meant nothing to me, but she didn't want to hear a word out of me. She walked away in such a huff that she didn't realize that molasses bits were spilling from her parcel.

I was desperate to find Aili today. During my lunch break, I walked over to the orphanage schoolyard, hoping to find Aili tending to the youngsters at their lunch recess. From behind the metal fence, I watched her as she played marbles with a small group of children. She looked like a child herself as she searched for the right marble from her leather pouch. Just as she was ready to toss her marble into the ring, she noticed me in her line of vision. She paused and excused herself from the game. I could not believe how beautiful she looked. My heart ached at her vision. The wind blew her dress tightly around her figure and revealed more than I or any man could stand. As she approached my spot at the fence, I exclaimed, "Aili, it's not what you think!" She slapped me before I could explain further. She stood there shocked at what she had done. Her eyes welled into tears and then she fell into my arms. I vow never to let Aili doubt my love again. When I left Aili, I saw Marian watching us from the hospital window. I pray that she'll keep what she witnessed to herself.

Another miner died today. Dominic Massucco was 50 years old. His wife and three children came to the office to berate Father in broken English. After about five minutes, she collapsed into a pile of grief. She didn't know how she would provide for her children. Father turned them out into the street, exclaiming loudly enough for the nearby strikers to hear, "Have those ingrates with the flags help you out! They seem to have enough money that they don't need to work." I waited a minute for Father to get settled once again in his office, and then I slipped out to find the widow and her children. I finally caught up with them outside Saint Anne's Catholic Church. "Please, come with me," I said. They followed me to Clara's boardinghouse. Clara agreed to take them in until better plans could be formalized. I thanked Clara and quickly got back to my office. I was shaking with fear, knowing that Father would disown me if he knew that I had helped the family. As I had just started to regain my composure, Father came in and gruffly asked, "Blanche Whitford tells me that you're dating an orphan from the Hennery. Would you like to tell me just what you think you're doing?"

After Father confronted me at the office yesterday, I asked if we could move the discussion to the Miscowaubik Club. The club's rich atmosphere always seemed to have a calming effect on Father, and, besides, I needed a drink. The club was crowded and the deep mahogany walls and plush carpets always reminds me of our wealth. I told Father how I had met Aili and how I've grown fond of her. I clarified her living arrangements with Clara and assured him that Clara's house wasn't a brothel. I even told him that her place has sometimes been known as a safe haven for widows and others down on their luck. Father listened intently, but never said a word until he was sure that I had finished. When I thought that I had done a decent job of declaring my position, and as he stirred his drink with his finger while watching the men at the nearby table playing cards, he said, "Either you quit seeing Aili, or you will be disowned by the family. What you have done is treasonous and jeopardizes our livelihood. I don't think that this matter requires further discussion."

After work today I found my way to Clara's boardinghouse. There were more people there than usual due to the fact that it was nearly the dinner hour. I found Clara in the kitchen preparing the main course. She was happy to see me and at my request went up the back servants' stairwell to summon Aili. After a few moments, Aili appeared. I asked for a private place to talk. With a concerned look on her face, she led me to her private room on the second floor. As Aili sat on her bed and I knelt on the floor, I described my dilemma. "But I'm not a member of the WFM," she cried. I told her as politely as I could that it was more than her position with the strikers. As her chin jutted out, I could tell that she knew that Father didn't approve of her position in life. I was crushed by the look on her face. "Oh Eston, what shall we do?" she wailed. She knew that I wasn't in a position to be disowned, and she knew that I had very strong feelings for her. "You must gain independence. You must write a successful play. It's the only way to break free!" she said with defiance. Knowing that it was just a way to buy time, I agreed that I would try to write something worthy and that, in the meantime, we'd have to see each other secretly.

Today was a big day for Red Jacket. The immortal Sarah Bernhardt was booked to perform *Camille* at the Red Jacket Opera House. Due to demand, tickets, aside from the C & H box seats, had been auctioned off at the City Drug Store. Mother and I had plans to go, so during late afternoon I secured our reserved box seat tickets from Al, the ticket seller, so that we would not have to wait in line prior to the performance. Father and I smoked cigars in his study before Mother and I left for the theater. He told me that a strike was imminent not only in Red Jacket, but also at all of the Keweenaw mines. He was happy that I was entertaining with Mother and hoped that I would meet a "fine" lady during intermission. Prior to the performance, we listened to the C & H Orchestra perform its preludes. The opera house is breathtaking. The opera house's plush velvet green carpet, accented by the crimson, gold and ivory color scheme rivals any in the United States. The copper chandelier, however, is the pride of Red Jacket. With over one hundred lights, it caught the gaze of most of the patrons until the lights dimmed. As the lights darkened, I noticed Marian and Judge Murphy's son in the box seats opposite ours. She gave me a sly grin as the lights went down.

Camille was superb, and Sarah Bernhardt captured the audience with her very first words. Once again, I could not concentrate during the performance. This time it was due to my activities during intermission. Bored with the conversation that Mother was having with her lady friends, I went wandering through the corridors of the opera house. Knowing that Aili was somewhere working as a wardrobe assistant, I found myself loitering in the basement where the dressing rooms were located. Just as the second act was to begin, I found Aili tending to Miss Bernhardt. As Miss Bernhardt made her ascent to stage level, Aili turned around to head back to the wardrobe room. She saw me and was shocked that I had found her. We embraced, and with hunger she pulled me into Miss Bernhardt's dressing room. For minutes we held each other close. We kissed passionately. We both had tears of happiness, as we longingly looked into each other eyes. With the start of the second act, I reluctantly had to make my way back to my box seats.

Luckily, Mother didn't say anything to Father about my mysterious disappearance at the theater. Father was already in a meeting with the C & H board of directors and Sheriff Cruse by the time I arrived to work today. Much to my surprise, about mid-morning, Aili showed up at my office in a fit of tears. Blanche Whitford had terminated Aili's volunteer status at the hospital. Apparently some vials of medicine, pain relievers, were missing from the pharmacy inventory. Marian told Blanche that Aili had been seen unattended in the pharmacy. Since volunteers are prohibited from entering the pharmacy, Blanche felt that Aili had to be dismissed from her duties. Obviously Marian's spite, caused by my lack of attention, was being directed towards Aili. "You'll get another job, Aili," I declared. She was not upset about the job. She was saddened that she couldn't help the people that really needed help, the miners and their children. Before I could console her further, I remembered that we were standing in the office, near Father. I quickly scooted Aili out the back entrance and promised to help rectify her situation.

Tensions are rising in Red Jacket. Father is unable to control the strikers any longer. Fight after fight keeps breaking out among the scabs and WFM members. The Red Jacket jail is so full with violators that the C & H armory has been made into a makeshift cellblock. One last declaration for truce telegram arrived from Charles Moyer. It was opened, discussed and quickly rejected by Father, the regional mine owners and various board members. The downtown merchants also mobilized at the administration building, demanding order and control. One last call to Judge Murphy was placed, but to no avail. Father dismissed the office early, stating that a strike was happening and that it would be best if people were in the safety of their own homes. In order to get home I had to fight my way through more than 200 miners, marching four abreast down Calumet Avenue. Among the cheering women and children I spotted Aili. I ran to her and pulled her out of the crowd. We ran off to the C & H Library on Red Jacket Road, far from the crowds. Once inside, we found our way to the basement game area, which also held public bathing rooms for men and women. Aili could not believe my devious idea to shower together, let alone at such a time of disorder. Frankly, neither could I.

The WFM's members decided to strike yesterday. Out of the 13,000 local miners, over 9,000 voted to strike. Over 500 miners stormed the mine, clubbing officials with rocks and picks. The mines were shut down, as were the mines in Houghton and Hancock. Father began to marshal his troops to meet the enemy. Telegram after telegram was sent to the state capital in Lansing. Bankers and shopkeepers vowed to support Father no matter what the cost. Their livelihoods were also at stake. Sheriff Cruse deputized more than 150 regular citizens to help keep the miners at bay and in their homes at night. I could not get to Aili today due to the uprising. I flush as I think of our risky encounter at the showers yesterday. Our passion far outweighed our fear of being caught. We stripped down to our undergarments and entered the womens' shower. The force of the shower caused Aili's hair twist to fall around her shoulders. As I kissed her, my hands found their way to her ample breasts. Through the muslin, I could feel her nipples harden at my touch. She too was searching with her hands as we kissed, and for a brief moment her virgin fingers paused on my manhood.

~ *WFM Headquarters, Calumet Miners' Union.* ~

The mine remained closed again today. Fights continued throughout the night between the scabs and strikers. The bars were shut down early at the sheriff's request. Arrests have been rampant, but the sentences don't seem to deter further outbreaks of aggression. Probably only one-fourth of the Red Jacket miners really want to strike. Many agree with the WFM's demands, but not enough to go on strike. Father and I met with those who refused to go on strike. Most are new immigrants and just happy to have any employment. They agreed to keep working, but they want extra protection on mine property as well as on the streets at night. Father telegrammed the state governor asking for military support. He claimed that the strikers were violent and jeopardized the livelihood of innocent citizens. The Governor agreed to send the state militia to Red Jacket. Unbelievable. Within five days 2,500 militiamen should arrive. Until then, Sheriff Cruse and his newly appointed deputies will try to keep the peace. They've even been authorized to carry firearms.

The mine opened today, but only to 20 percent capacity. More than 400 striking miners rallied outside the entrance to the mine. Aside from a few scabs getting pushed or having their lunch pail grabbed from them, the rally was peaceful. Father and I spent most of the day meeting with bankers and merchants. They agreed to create the Citizens' Alliance in order to help C & H regain control of the strike. They also started a newspaper titled *Truth* to spread their version of the strike issues to the non-strikers and regular citizens. Members are to wear white Citizens' Alliance buttons to show their support. I helped to deliver membership applications to all of the businesses in Red Jacket, Laurium and Calumet. I think that most merchants are joining out of fear. Since C & H owns most of the banks in town, merchants fear that their credit will be cut off if they don't join the alliance. I was ashamed to enter McGrath's with an application. Clara could not believe that I could be a member of such a group. "Family or no family, your involvement with this group is unacceptable to me as I'm sure it is to Aili. You'll eventually have to choose your position. Right now you're walking the fence to keep your family happy. What about Aili? What about me? What about the widows and children?" With that, Clara tore up the flyer and asked me to leave her bar.

Clara's words stung yesterday. She was right. I'm a horrible coward, unable to stand for what I think is right. I'm not sure if I even know what's right or wrong. How can I challenge Father and the only way of life that I know? How would I provide for myself? I know that only a select few make a successful living at writing plays. How could I provide for a wife and family? Is it so bad that our money provides housing, libraries, opera houses and commerce for the people of Red Jacket? I wanted to see Aili to discuss my feelings, but was afraid that she may have already heard about the alliance movement. Not knowing where to go or where to turn, I headed straight to a tavern. Since I didn't dare go to McGrath's, I picked Vairo's, a pub near the Italian section of Red Jacket. I felt as if I were in a foreign country. Italian miners and scabs came and went without knowing my position. I was alone with my thoughts when I felt a tap on my shoulder. As I turned around, I came face to face with a fist of an Italian striker. I awakened today in a hospital bed and with Marian tending to my injuries.

I was startled to find myself in the hospital yesterday. I'm not sure if my head hurt more from the hangover or the concussion. Marian couldn't have been happier to see me in such a predicament. She told me that my parents visited me earlier but had gone on to church. She told me that they were very upset by my decision to visit a bar, let alone during the miners' strike. As Marian was folding linens near the window, she exclaimed, "Look at the strikers today, all dressed in their Sunday best!" I wrapped myself in a sheet and staggered to the window to see for myself. She was right. Even the ladies and children were dressed up and adorned with ribbons. "Oh look! There's Aili! Doesn't she look just beautiful?" Marion said with sarcasm. I thanked her for pointing out the obvious and quickly got dressed behind the dressing screen. As she left the room she said, "Don't be shy, Eston, it's nothing I haven't seen before. Who do you think undressed you last night?" I'm really beginning to hate that woman. I left the hospital without getting the physician's approval. The sun and extreme heat made me feel weak. I could see Aili, but before I could catch up with her I fainted just outside of St. Anne's Cathedral. This time Father and Mother found me as they left the church.

After Father and Mother found me passed out on the church steps, they helped me home to my own bed. When I did come to, my father did not waste a minute before chastising me for my behavior. "What were you thinking?" he said. "Don't you realize that we are the enemy, that we are hated? They see us as the cause for their demise. You must remember your place and your priorities." After Father left, Mother came in and sat by my bedside. She handed me a note from Aili. She told me that she understood my feelings for Aili and that she wouldn't tell Father about the note. She left me alone so that I could have some privacy to read the note. It read:

> My dearest Eston,
> I hope that this note finds you well. Clara told me about the Citizens' Alliance as well as your mishap at Vairo's. I don't want to come between you, C & H and your family. You must do what's right for you, and I must do what's right for Clara, the miners and myself. I hope that beneath the surface you know what's right. I understand your predicament, but I hope that truth will prevail and reunite our lives sometime in the future.
>
> Lovingly yours,
> Aili

I stayed home from the office today. My head still hurts, and I'm still wallowing in self-pity. Headache or heartache, my father didn't care. He sent me to the C & H armory to prepare it for the arrival of the state militia. Since the makeshift jail was overflowing with violators, I had to make arrangements for the militia to set up camp outside on the armory grounds. I can't believe the state feels our situation is so bad that it warrants militia support. True, a few fights have broken out and the strikers have paraded every day for a week now, but I think that Father and the business owners have exaggerated the conditions to the governor. Needless to say, by nightfall, with the help of Tamarack General Goods, I prepared the grounds with temporary lighting, power generators and food supplies. The strikers, having heard about the militia's orders, rallied near the grounds all day. With help from the sheriff's deputies, many had retreated to their homes by nightfall. Uncertain what tomorrow's arrival of the militia may bring, I'm making it an early night too. Already I miss seeing Aili.

General Abby and the militia arrived in Red Jacket around 2 p.m. today. Everyone was awestruck at how quickly they converted the C & H armory and Red Jacket itself to a military base. Tents were placed on every street corner, even church lawns and mine entrances. General Abby and the higher-ranking officials have made arrangements to stay at the Copper Range Hotel, our finest sleeping facility. After securing his quarters, the general met with Sheriff Cruse, Father and some Citizens' Alliance members to discuss the next course of action. It was agreed that roadblocks would be placed on all avenues leading to the area mines. The strikers met this challenge with anger. Already the militia troops have been cursed at and stoned by the strikers. Once the general and his men got the strikers into their homes for the evening, they retired to the Miscowaubik Club for spirits. Father and I, out of courtesy, joined them and found ourselves toasting, with champagne, to their first successful day. After far too many toasts, we had to help General Abby and his top officer, Lt. Col. Shotwell, find their way back to the Copper Range Hotel.

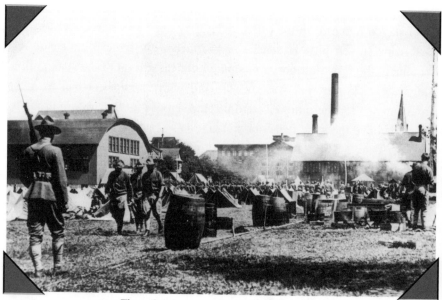

∼ The militia's camp just outside the armory. ∼

Today the County Board of Commissioners, which includes Father, agreed to hire 50 strikebreakers from a New York company called Waddell-Mahon. The "waddies," as they are called, will be authorized to carry guns while they try to keep the strikers in line. Including the Citizens' Alliance members, the sheriff has pulled together nearly 3000 armed men to hold back the strikers. With such a force present, most of the area mines were able to open to partial capacity. We hosted a dinner tonight for the Whitfords, Cruses, General Abby and Lt. Col. Shotwell. Marion's brother, James, was quite impressed by General Abby and his career. We could not get him to stop asking so many questions of the general. After several glasses of wine, it became apparent that Marian had shifted her attentions away from me to Lt. Col. Shotwell. I couldn't blame her for being unable to resist a man in uniform. Even though twice her age, the lieutenant seems to be smitten with Marian. Perhaps he'll be able to tame her wicked tongue. After dessert and more wine, the party broke up. The lieutenant offered to walk Marian home. I was relieved that I was not burdened with the task.

~ General Abby and some of his men. ~

It rained all day today. In addition to the rain, there was a fierce north wind. The wind was a reminder that fall isn't too far away. Even in the inclement weather, the strikers were out in force. From my office window I saw Big Annie get pushed to the ground by a waddie as she tried to break through a roadblock. It was not a pretty sight watching Big Annie and the thug from New York wrestle in the mud. The whole while Big Annie seemed to manage to keep her twelve-foot flag held high for all to see. Big Annie was arrested and taken to the armory, but Judge Murphy quickly released her with a warning for trespassing. This evening, once all was quiet, the forces retired to their tents or hit one of the 50 available bars in Red Jacket. Never has Red Jacket seen so much commotion. A prostitution ring, which followed the militia to Red Jacket from Lansing, has helped to keep every hotel room in Red Jacket packed to capacity. By morning Sheriff Cruse claims that he'll have them rounded up and back on a train to Lansing. Some of the men were told about Clara's boardinghouse. I tried to stop some from going there, but to no avail. I was told that Clara and Aili fought some militiamen off their doorstep with a broom and some choice words. I pray that Clara and Aili survive this mess.

It was a beautiful August day today. The sky was blue and filled with large, puffy cumulous clouds. The clouds passed by quickly because of the slight north wind that was blowing. It was probably only 70 degrees or so, but still a perfect Upper Michigan day. The strikers were fairly quiet today except for their morning and evening parade around the mine entrances. The guardsmen were eager to establish calm among the strikers so that they could catch the evening trolley to Electric Park, a wooded park located between Red Jacket and Houghton. The Red Jacket Municipal Band and others were performing at the park's dance pavilion. I joined General Abby and Lt. Col. Shotwell on the trolley to the park. It was apparent that the general and his fellow officers had already had too much to drink. They talked about nothing but finding some ladies to perform ungentlemanly acts upon. I had to laugh at the way they discussed such a delicate subject. Once off the trolley I fell behind the officers so that I could roam the grounds on my own.

I was afraid to be associated with the officers in their state of drunkenness. I spotted Aili and Clara having a picnic dinner, but I chose to leave them alone tonight. With the militiamen and Marian present, it was best to leave well enough alone. It's pleasure enough just to be able to write outside and enjoy the sound of the bands.

August 4, 1913

Once again a new day has greeted me with a headache. After Marian found me at the park last night, she first chastised me for longing for Aili, and then she dragged me to the dance floor. Her sole purpose was to get closer to Lt. Col. Shotwell, who also was present on the dance floor, but with another lady. The booze was in abundance, and at one point I found myself drinking bootleg prune whiskey. Even Marian was drinking to impress the lieutenant. The last thing that I remember was seeing Marian and the lieutenant disappear into the woods. Apparently I passed out on my blanket and Marian some how got me back on the trolley to Red Jacket. She woke me up once again as the trolley approached the Calumet Avenue stop. Still drunk, somehow I escorted Marian home. This morning as I got dressed I noticed a crumpled piece of paper lying on the floor next to my shoes. It was a note from Aili asking me to meet her at her mother's gravesite at noon today.

◦ Another evening of fun at Electric Park. ◦

I guess I didn't realize just how much I have missed Aili. We sat and conversed in the cemetery until late afternoon yesterday. She told me about her mother and father's struggle to come to the United States from Finland. They arrived to Ellis Island in the spring of 1896. Upon their arrival, her father was quarantined because of an eye virus. Her mother was met by relatives and went on to Red Jacket without her father. Her father never made it to Red Jacket. He was sent back to Finland on a ship, where he caught a fever. He died before reaching his homeland. Aili's mother found herself pregnant and alone. Clara took her in when her relatives were no longer able to provide for her. Her mother died during Aili's birth, and Clara has been caring for her ever since. We reclined on the lawn and watched the clouds pass as we shared our dreams.

My visit with Aili yesterday was interrupted by gunfire. The gunfire came from the guards at Shaft No. 2. Apparently a miner broke through the barricades and was on the loose on mine property. The guards caught up with him as he approached the shaft. They had to shoot into the air to get him to come out from behind the shaft. They found two sticks of dynamite in his pocket. The striking miner claimed that he had forgotten to remove them from his jacket after he had been in the woods clearing and preparing trees for firewood. The guards didn't believe him, so he was taken to jail and charged with trespassing and with intent to cause property damage. Father and I have been asked to meet with a committee of miners who want to go back to work. Apparently, over 1000 miners have signed a non-union list and would like to meet with Father and me to discuss their demands. Father doesn't like the sounds of it, but he's agreed to meet with the committee tomorrow. Sheriff Cruse arrived at our offices just as we were about to call it a day. He brought the news that a miner had been accidentally shot by a militia guard as he exited the Wolverine Mine entrance. It seems that the militia's presence is causing more harm than good.

We arrived at work today with news that over 200 miners have stormed the militia at Wolverine. Such melee was all that Mother Jones, a fierce fighter for American labor, needed to gain further support for her visit to Red Jacket. She arrived at the Red Jacket Depot and was greeted by a crowd of over 2,000. Father sent me to the Palestra Rink in Laurium as a spy to hear her words. She urged the strikers to hang tough, remain peaceful and stand together. The crowd cheered Mother Jones as they left the rink. Some of the strikers jeered and stoned the militia guarding the rink. I followed the parading miners back to Red Jacket. I was amazed at the different nationalities that were represented. Differences aside, they all seemed to understand what they wanted from the mine owners. Everybody seems to understand money. Aili found me in the crowd. She walked with me as long as she could. As I stopped to enter the Red Jacket Hall, the meeting place of the newly formed non-striker committee, Aili asked if I would meet her at her mother's grave again on Sunday. I grabbed and kissed her delicate fingers as I told her that I would be counting the hours until then.

⁓ Mother Jones during her visit to the strike zone. ⁓

The meeting at the Red Jacket Hall was a non-productive one. Father felt that their demands were no different or in some cases worse than those of WFM members. Not only did they want an eight-hour workday, but also they wanted double time, not time and a half, for overtime and Sundays. They also wanted C & H to hire young men, less than 18 years of age, to act as lookouts for falling rocks as the miners work the one-man drill. Absurd! We left the meeting abruptly because a WFM striker ran into the hall ranting and raving in Finnish and broken English to try to convince the non-strikers to strike. Once we returned to the office, we received a telegram from Governor Ferris ordering the withdrawal of the militia because he concluded that the deputies and the militia were responsible for most of the violence. "Damn!" shouted Father. "The strikers will surely see this as a victory. We must gather new forces." He sent me out to find Sheriff Cruse and Judge Murphy. Outside the office the strikers were thick in number and jubilant from hearing the news of the militia withdrawal. I feared for my life and my future as I worked my way home through the unruly crowd.

Last night Father and I met with Sheriff Cruse, Judge Murphy and General Abby at the club. General Abby agreed to reduce the militia gradually, instead of a complete withdrawal. Judge Murphy pleaded with Father to meet with Charles Moyer. He absolutely refused, as did some of the other local mine owners. Sheriff Cruse, now in charge of organizing protection, called for the employment of strikebreakers from the Ascher Detective Agency in New York. After some sort of plan was in place, Father and Judge Murphy retired for the evening. General Abby, Lt. Col. Shotwell and I stayed after to enjoy one last cigar and brandy. The general talked wildly about his accusers, which included Governor Ferris and WFM officers. "They won't provide me with any proof of the drunken meandering and militia outrages," he slurred. With each additional drink he got louder and more adamant of his prowess as a leader. "Females in jeopardy? I've got proof that Red Jacket's finest throw themselves at us, not the other way around!" he declared. "Just look at Marian Whitford! Lt. Col. Shotwell here claims that she's insatiable!" Shocked at where this conversation was headed, I quickly suggested that we call it a night.

Father and I were shocked to find out that over 2,000 striking miners, mostly single men, have already left Red Jacket for work elsewhere. The ticket clerk at the Red Jacket Depot claims that most are headed for Detroit, where Henry Ford is paying $5 per day compared to our $2.50. Due to a short supply of workers, Father and I had to go down into the mine to help supervise the trammers loading rocks. Afterward Father was as determined as ever to import more workers. After dinner I took a stroll down Fifth Street. The militia as usual was out enjoying the sounds of the Red Jacket Municipal Band. The band has finally raised enough funds to purchase their new red uniforms. Now they look as good as they sound. I saw Marian and Lt. Col. Shotwell enter the Rock Building Saloon on Sixth Street. Apparently he has to see Marian just one more time before he has to leave Red Jacket. I went to McGrath's. Aili was tending the bar in place of Clara. I sat and listened to Aili as she told me about how Clara was raped and beaten by one of General Abby's men.

~ The Red Jacket Municipal Band showing off their new uniforms. ~

I went to visit Clara today at the boardinghouse. I could not believe her condition. Her face is completely distorted. I hardly recognized her. She cannot talk because her jaw was broken. She shook her head to tell me that it wasn't my fault. In her eyes I could see that she didn't believe it. I reassured her that things were going to get better because the militia has been ordered to leave and that the strike will surely be over in no time at all. After my visit with Clara, I found myself at the opera house looking for Aili. I knew that she'd be there because tonight is the opening of *Peter Pan*, starring Maude Adams. As I suspected, Aili was hard at work putting the finishing touches on the lead's costume. We played hide and seek like children, running carelessly from dressing room to dressing room. We even lifted ourselves to stage level with the rising trap door. We pretended to act out my play, one that I made up as we went along. Aili found it quite amusing and told me to rewrite it because I surely wouldn't be able to support her with my current work.

Today, I met Aili at her mother's grave. We hiked to the woods surrounding Tamarack Park and picked blueberries until we couldn't hold anymore in our pails. We warmed ourselves in the sun and ate blueberries until our teeth became blue. We parted, not knowing when we'd steal another moment together.

Today, over 50 percent of the militia left Red Jacket. Sheriff Cruse was officially put in charge of keeping order among the rioting miners. He ordered riot sticks the size of baseball bats from a nearby lumber company. Once the strikebreakers arrive from New York, he'll have over 3,000 armed men left to patrol the mines of Keweenaw and Houghton counties. Father had me compile output reports from C & H, as well as from ten regional subsidiary companies. Clearly, the Lake Superior properties have been affected by the labor troubles. Total July output was down from June's output by over 2.5 million pounds. This, combined with increased competition and the general drop of the price of copper per pound, isn't painting a prosperous picture for our future. Father figures that C & H will only be prosperous for another ten years. The cost of going deeper to get quality copper is costing the company too much to keep up with the external forces from the competition. Ten years too long for me. Father keeps talking about making me the Assistant Mine Captain, second in command after him. I really don't want his headaches. I'm fine, number crunching and dreaming about my future away from the mines.

August 14, 1913

The Fireman's Tournament, involving several hundred Upper Michigan firemen, was held in Red Jacket today. Part of the festivities included eight marching bands and the sponsorship of the Miller Carnival Company. Due to the large number of townspeople out enjoying the tournament and carnival rides, the strikers got great visibility as they paraded along Depot Street and Calumet Avenue. By 4:30 today the strikers' parade erupted into a mob. Father and I were called to Shaft No. 2 where the unruly strikers were holding several "deputized" employees and Captain William Kievela, the mine engineer, hostage. They first ripped the deputy stars from the employees' shirts and then held the Captain and his employees at gunpoint. They wouldn't let the captain bring the workers up from beneath the surface. Father and I negotiated with them that once the workers were up, then no more would be allowed down, but that two or three engineers were needed to work in the boiler house to monitor the steam pressure on the pumps. If the pumps were shut down, the mine would fill with water. The strikers moved on to the "dry," or changing house, after they were satisfied that Shaft No. 2 had been shut down. Here they jeered and kicked at the workers as they changed out of their work clothes.

August 15, 1913

After an exhausting night at the mine, Father and I awoke to news from Sheriff Cruse that several of the other local mines have also been shut down at gunpoint. Sheriff Cruse was injured himself by a blow to the head with a blunt pipe. It seems that a warrant has been issued for two strikers who held the engineers at gunpoint. Sheriff Cruse named the strikers as Kollan and

Pashquan who live in a boardinghouse in Seeberville. Sheriff Cruse and several waddies plan on arresting them tomorrow on grounds of intimidation. After an unsuccessful try at keeping Father calm, I ventured out to the carnival to see if I could find Aili. I found her escorting some children from the orphanage. She had the head schoolmistress attend to them while we stole a ride on the ferris wheel. As we rode, I filled her in on the latest happenings at the mine and about the Seeberville warrants. As we talked, we enjoyed the view from the ferris wheel. Red Jacket never looked so beautiful. The red mine stone buildings stood out magnificently among the dark blue water of Lake Superior.

~ *The scabs waiting to be brought up to the surface by the man-car.* ~

The arrest in Seeberville did not go as planned. Sheriff Cruse assigned the arrest to Deputy Sheriff Polkinghorne, three men from Wadell-Mahon and two county peace officers. When they arrived at the boardinghouse, they found Kollan and Pashquan out in the yard drunk and playing Tenpins with some of the other boarders. After the deputy said that the two strikers were under arrest, the other boarders backed into the house. Nobody knows what happened next, but shots were fired and two ended up dead. Steve Putrich and Dlazig Tazen, a 17-year-old boy, were found dead on the second floor stairwell. Witnesses claim that Tazen was shot on the first floor but climbed to the second floor, as he exclaimed, "By God, they've killed me," only to die in Putrich's arms. A baby in her mother's arms was also grazed in the face by a stray bullet. Sheriff Cruse arrived at the scene to investigate. Warrants were initially issued for the gunmen, but they escaped to an adjoining county shortly after the incident. Sheriff Cruse has not pursued them yet. Father was furious at the news and instructed Sheriff Cruse to report to the public that the shots were fired from within the boardinghouse, implying that a striker's gun must have killed its own.

The two Houghton County peace officers have been arrested for murder, but the four imported deputies from Waddell-Mahon have not been found. Father and I fought all day with our local prosecuting attorney and county board. The prosecuting attorney, at the insistence of Charles Moyer, plans to serve papers on Sheriff Cruse and James Waddell, which would prohibit them from employing any other outside deputies. Because of this, Father and the county board are insisting on an outside prosecutor to handle the strike cases. Joseph Cannon, organizer for the WFM, is planning a public funeral at the Palestra on Sunday. Father is furious that the WFM is moving the bodies by a special funeral train from Painesdale to Laurium. The train has plans to stop at all intermediate stations so that different parties of strikers can get on board. After lunch Father summoned Sheriff Cruse and James Waddell to our office to discuss securing the mines during Sunday's funeral. By early evening we still hadn't seen any sign of Sheriff Cruse or Waddell, so Father sent me out in the new Ford to search for them. I returned home without a sighting of the missing men.

I searched for Sheriff Cruse and James Wadell until 9 p.m. last night. I couldn't find them anywhere, and they never responded to Father's messages. Before I returned the Ford, I drove by Clara's in search of Aili. She had never ridden in an automobile, so I thought that I'd surprise her with a drive to the shore. Clara greeted me at the door. She still had black and blue marks on her face from her unnamed and unpunished guardsman. She was more reserved than usual, probably because of the Seeberville murders. She led me to Aili, who was behind the boardinghouse, tending to her food garden. She dropped her basket of fresh tomatoes as she ran to greet me. She was very nervous about riding in the Ford, but seemed to be amazed by the beautiful piece of machinery. The sunset was spectacular as was the company.

It appeared that every striker in the district participated in the funeral of Dlazig Tazan and Steven Putrich. The procession from the Palestra to St. John's Croatian Church was the biggest funeral demonstration ever known in Houghton County. At the Lakeview Cemetery gravesite, Joseph Cannon, organizer for the local WFM, gave an impassioned speech and censured the mine owners and stockholders for the killings. He declared that the miners should try to remain peaceful in the future. This would ensure the removal of the troops. Sheriff Cruse and James Waddell finally reached Father today. They had been hiding out in Houghton to avoid the injunction proceedings. They figure that the strike's end is near and that the injunction will then be irrelevant. Due to the mass exodus of Croatian workers, Father placed a call to Ellis Island in search of immigrants not matching Finnish or Croatian descent. He agrees that the end of the strike may be near because many strikers are coming back asking for their original jobs. He feels that with so many flocking back, that the C & H shafts may be hoisting within two days.

Confident that the strike is almost over, Sheriff Cruse and Wadell returned to Red Jacket today. They were served their papers, but the proceeding won't be scheduled until October or November. In celebration for their win against the WFM, Father, Sheriff Cruse, James Waddell, General Abby, Lt. Col. Shotwell and I met at the club for dinner. Talks centered on the fact that the WFM only has $23,000 of the $800,000 necessary to keep the strike going. Not one cent of the promised $3.00 a day for each striker has been paid out by the federation. We discussed allowing for the eight-hour day, but have no intentions of implementing it for months because we don't want to appear as if we're giving in to WFM demands. As the booze flowed, the talk turned to women. Lt. Col. Shotwell had also been at the shore with Marian the night I drove Aili there. In front of Father, the lieutenant asked me about the blond sitting next to me in the Ford. Father broke his conversation with General Abby to give me one of his looks. I'm sure that we'll be discussing the matter further.

Father had me in his office by 8 a.m. to discuss my whereabouts last Saturday evening. I confessed to him that I had been with Aili. He called her a radical socialist Finn. He declared that the Finns were behind this whole strike and that he would not stand for my behavior one more minute. He gave me another warning about being disowned if I was ever seen with Aili again. He was so impassioned and furious that this time I almost believe him. His ranting was cut short by the arrival of Sheriff Cruse. He had come with the news that the WFM had finally come through with financial and ration support for the miners. Over 4,000 gathered at the Palestra. According to reports, the South Range, Hancock and Keweenaw mines have showed huge numbers not reporting to work. Apparently our celebration last night was premature. It now appears that the strike has gained strength. The sheriff also reported that the WFM would be setting up co-op stores throughout the district where miners would use coupons, instead of cash, to buy groceries and supplies. This will surely infuriate the Citizens' Alliance group, made up of mostly local shop owners. Their business is down enough because of the strike. This will only make matters worse.

The Coroner's inquest into the cause of the Seeberville deaths began today. All six deputies charged with the murders have been taken into custody by the sheriff and were present at the Houghton hearings. The strikers outside the courtroom were, as a rule, orderly during the preliminary hearing. General Abby assured Sheriff Cruse that the state military board and Governor Ferris would not recall the remaining troops as long as there was any possibility of trouble or interference with the mine operations. At mine headquarters today, the federation had large numbers of picketers on duty. At one point, the guards had to use their riot sticks to disperse the crowds. The women were out in large numbers also trying to get the strikers, who had decided to return to work, to rejoin the union. Many refused to rejoin because they thought that their wages were fair and that enough damage had been done. Many also couldn't survive on WFM's partial payment of what was due to them. It's said that one striker, whose wife had deserted him, had no option but to return to work. On his first day back, he locked his one-year-old babe in the house and his two-year-old son in a shed. Both children were found in pitiful condition and were placed in the care of a charitable family.

With the rebirth of the strike, I've hardly had time to think about my predicament with Aili. I spoke to Mother about it briefly this morning at breakfast. She's advised me to follow Father's wishes, mainly because she fears that he really might disown me from the family and any future wealth. She encouraged me to pursue writing plays but chastised me for not working at my passion diligently. She's absolutely correct. I enjoy writing, but I lack a defined focus. I seriously doubt that I could support myself with my writings. I departed for work in a foul mood. It wasn't quite as foul as the weather. It poured rain most of the day, and the temperature barely made the low sixties. I'm sure that the cold nights and thoughts of winter coming will induce many of the strikers back to work. I pray that the strike ends soon. Perhaps if it does, Father will relent on his feelings toward Aili. Thoughts of Aili always melt away any of my loyalties to family or wealth accumulation.

Last night Sheriff Cruse called on us to tell us about a clash at the Red Jacket Depot. With the arrival of the last train from Houghton, the strikers attacked the imported workers as they exited the train. Over 30 workers were injured and taken to the hospital for treatment. With John Mitchell, Vice President of the American Federation of Labor, arriving to the area on Saturday, Father asked Sheriff Cruse if he could get General Abby to secure more troops in the Copper Country. The deportation of so many of the guardsmen seems premature now. I went to the hospital to see how many of the injured imported men would be ready for work on Monday. Since many of our workers joined the WFM after it made its first payment to the stikers, we're once again in need of underground men. Marian was on duty, but she ignored me as I made my request of Blanche. As I was leaving, Marian impatiently asked if Lt. Col. Shotwell was expected back to the area any time soon. She looked anxious but relieved as I told her that I thought that he would most definitely arrive sometime this weekend. His supervision is needed during John Mitchell's address to the strikers.

Mother arrived home for lunch in tears. She was over 30 minutes late to meet Father and me because she could not stop herself from watching the spectacle at the Red Jacket Depot. She said that over 1,000 children were being put on trains to Marquette because their parents were no longer able to keep them fed and safe due to the strike. She said that hundreds of parents were at the station sobbing as their children were being sent away temporarily, but in all likelihood forever. Mother asked Father if there was anything that could be done to help the families. Father scolded Mother and reminded her that her place in life was not to ask questions. I told Father that I would go to the depot to check out the situation. At the depot, I saw Aili for the first time in nearly a week. I watched her strength as she comforted parents and crying children. The sight was haunting. How could C & H cause such strife, especially since it's provided all of Red Jacket's citizens with the finest jobs, buildings and commerce? Humiliated, I left the depot before Aili could notice me.

There were no parades today. Obviously, the WFM's showing at John Mitchell's address was display enough. The back-to-work movement will certainly be delayed. Mitchell did not help the strike situation. He even quoted Abraham Lincoln by saying "Thank God, we have a system of labor that allows the American workingman to go on a strike." He went on to say, "This is your fight, but nevertheless the struggle of labor here is the struggle of labor everywhere. I bring you a message of sympathy and support and bid you stand fast until the victory is won." We also had a setback in regards to our hiring of guards from Waddell and Mahon. Judge Murphy declared that he would not issue an order to restrain us from hiring the guards, but he said that the guards must conduct themselves within the law. This would include not breaking up peaceful parades. Neither the sheriff nor anyone of his employ will be allowed to break a strike. Such discretion is a victory for the strikers. The presence of the Waddell-Mahon guards will not convey the same strength as it once did. Depressed that the strike's end is nowhere in sight, I went to find Aili at her mother's grave. She was not there, but she did leave me a note, which asked me to meet her at Electric Park for a wedding celebration tomorrow.

Today I met Aili at Electric Park. Her cousin's wedding ceremony was already over by the time I arrived, but the picnic and music were in full swing. The bride's beauty was nothing in comparison to Aili's. Aili was wearing her best Sunday dress of white, and she even had flowers woven through her hair. We tried to forget the strike as we danced and enjoyed the celebration. I didn't have the heart to tell her about Father's demands until we were on the last trolley back to Red Jacket. I told her that I thought with the strike's end, Father might change his mind about our relationship, but in the meantime we'd have to carefully plan our meetings. Aili talked about how hurt she's been by seeing so many families broken up by the strike. Clara has even taken in several children until their parents can better provide for them. Aili has never blamed me for the strike, but her strength and sympathy for the strikers always makes me feel greedy and unsympathetic. I told Aili that there was no use fighting over something that we couldn't change. She corrected me by saying "...or that you're unwilling to change."

It was not a good day in Copper Country. The soldiers and deputies were told by General Abby to prepare for a battle with the strikers. By midnight last night there was a general order for every soldier and deputy sheriff in service in the strike district to report to duty by 5:30 this morning. It was believed that the strikers were prepared to resort to arms, if need be, in order to shut down all shafts currently in operation. As it turned out, the striking miners did not cross the strike lines, but rather they held parades in both the north and south ends of the region. In the north end, the strikers formed at Mohawk, and in the south, at South Range. A feature of the parades was that every striker had his family with him. Since the women and children were present, normal restrictive measures were hampered. Sheriff Cruse ordered the guards to lay long lines of fire hose in the road to be used in case of trouble. Once the children and women were out of the way, further disturbances were to be quelled by normal tactics. Luckily, the strikers did not cross the line. Perhaps they were testing the waddies to see if they'd resort to the violence prohibited by Judge Murphy. By day's end, the crowds had retreated and the region remained quiet.

After Father and I had supper at the club last night, we returned home to find a bomb planted under our front porch. The bomb consisted of dynamite with a cap and fuse attached. We, including Mother, who was hysterical, immediately left the house. We went to Sheriff Cruse's office at the jail. He was helping the other guards serve dinner to the inmates when we arrived. Our mouths dropped as we saw the people he was serving. Large numbers of women and children were behind every cell door. Apparently as the men were leaving the underground at the end of their shift, they were pelted with rotten eggs and rocks. The militia had trouble breaking up the wives of the strikers because many of them were armed with the above-mentioned missiles as well as broomsticks dipped in human excrement. Because the children refused to leave their mothers as they were arrested, the entire group was thrown into jail. Sheriff Cruse promised to call upon General Abby as soon as things got under control at the jail. After some deputies secured our house, we returned home. Lying near the front steps was a sign that read JAMES HARLOW–THE AGITATOR.

Mother has made plans to leave for Grand Haven to stay with her sister until the strike gets resolved. The bomb threat was just too much for her to handle. Father and I, along with several other regional mine owners, met with Judge Murphy today to map out terms under which the mine operators will consider a settlement to the strike. The operators agree that membership in the WFM will not bar any man from returning to work, but they reserve the right to refuse employment to any agitator who has been guilty of violence or disorder. They also will insist upon the complete withdrawal of the federation from the strike district. The operators will consider a shorter workday, but they will not allow for the discontinuance of the one-man drill due to the low grade rock remaining to be mined. Judge Murphy will present the terms to Governor Ferris at his home in Big Rapids on Friday. After our meeting I retreated to McGrath's for some spirits. Both Clara and Aili were working behind the bar. Clara allowed Aili to take a break, so we talked for a few minutes before Clara called her back to work.

After his conference with Judge Murphy, Governor Ferris said, "I do not hesitate to say that the men have real grievances. By this I do not want to be understood as taking the position that they are right in all their contentions and should have all the concessions they demand, but they are entitled to some of the things they ask and this fact, in my opinion, makes the position taken by the operators seem arrogant and unfair. You can say for me that as long as the presence of the soldiers in the Copper Country is necessary to afford protection to the life and property of any man who desires to work, they will remain on the job." Father was furious with Governor Ferris' statement. Father and the other mine owners have refused and will continue to refuse to negotiate or recognize the federation. In retaliation for not reaching a settlement, the area operators agreed to evict any striker from company homes on September 1st unless they return to work. Guy Miller, of the executive board of the federation stated the following news: "We will stick to the finish…that the operators will deal with the men collectively through our organization. No money, no food, now no shelter. The will of the people has been spoken."

Father and I put Mother on a train to Grand Haven today. She was a bundle of nerves and in tears as she said her good-byes. As she hugged me, she whispered, "Obey your father and love Aili from afar until the strike is finished." The depot was filled with striking miners awaiting the arrival of Charles Moyer. He arrived later today from Denver. He plans on addressing what's expected to be thousands of miners at the Palestra in Laurium tomorrow. As we left the crowded station, some miners' wives accosted us. We were lucky to escape to our car before getting seriously injured. I dropped Father off at the office and went on to Houghton to check out the County Fair. After checking out the livestock displays, I went on to the produce area where I purchased some fresh vegetables to deliver to Clara and Aili. Since fresh produce is difficult to find in the winter months, I'm sure that Aili and Clara will preserve most of them for later. Aili was at the theater when I delivered the food, but Clara seemed touched by my thoughtfulness. As I headed home, I saw Marian leaving the armory in a fit of tears. Perhaps Lt. Col. Shotwell has had his fill of her.

Over 2,700 people met at the Palestra to hear Charles Moyer's address. Moyer's speech characterized the eight-hour workday as the vital issue of the strike, as well as the right of miners to organize and demand recognition. He also called upon all domestic and international unions to appropriate substantial amounts of aid for the copper miners. With the promise of aid, many miners, who had recently gone back to work, decided to rejoin the movement. Since it was so hot today, I eavesdropped on Moyer's speech from the outside of the Palestra. It was also a much safer vantage point should some striker recognize me. After I had heard enough, I went to find Aili at our usual Sunday meeting place. She was waiting anxiously for my arrival. "Have you heard? Have you heard?" she exclaimed. "Marion is pregnant and Lt. Col. Shotwell has denied being the father and he's left town!" This news clearly explains what I saw yesterday. Marian had obviously confronted the lieutenant and didn't like his response. As much as I despise Marian, I do feel sorry that she must now face raising a child alone and give up on any career plans that she may have had. Such a scandal!

Father and I worked out of our home today, Labor Day. We knew that the striker mobs would be out in full force today, especially because of the holiday and the fine fall weather. Sheriff Cruse came to dinner tonight. We discussed the inquisition of Cruse and his men and also the likelihood that the schools wouldn't open on time because so many miners can't afford to pay for children's books and clothes. I could only think of Aili during this conversation because we had already discussed the miners' hardship and the overall effect the strike would have on the children, the innocent ones. Father's paternalistic ranting seems so shallow compared to Aili's passionate sympathy for the miners. Sheriff Cruse told us about an incident at the North Kearsarge mine, two miles north of Calumet. Apparently the striker followed some scabs as they got off their shift and tried to push them out into the street. The deputies joined forces to protect the miners, and the strikers pressed against them. In doing so, the deputies fired. One of the shots struck and killed a fourteen-year-old girl.

The schools did open today but not with the usual number of students. Instead of having different classes for different levels of aptitude, the main school went back to a one-room classroom format. Father reminded the striking miners that they could send their children to the free night classes offered by C & H should they want to have their children taught at night. There were many other accounts of trouble throughout the copper fields yesterday. The 94 degree Indian summer day did not help tempers. The Quincy Mine and Copper Range Railroad both reported violence, largely brought on by women. Two men were beat up by women at the railroad station, and over 1,000 paraded in Calumet after attacking a guard at the armory. General Abby's men had to shoot into the crowd to break up a mob of women who had taken off their shoes and hurled them at the working miners as they walked home from their shift. Father and I supervised the installation of a searchlight on the C & H water tower. It will be used to detect prowlers on company property. We have been told that it should throw a light as far as Ahmeek, twenty-five miles away.

Father, our company lawyer and I waited all day for a call from Governor Ferris. We knew that he was meeting with Charles Moyer today to discuss possible resolutions to the strike. The call never came. After we dined at the club, I set out to find Aili under the premise that I was going down to Fifth Street to hear the band. Clara told me that I could find Aili at the cattle yard tending to their milking cow. Aili was a sight. Her hair was disheveled and her clothes soiled by the yard's red dust. I blushed as she pulled at the cows udders. She's even beautiful doing the most mundane tasks. She found it amusing that I've never milked a cow. I waited for her in the stacks at the library as she went below to wash in the public bath. I'm proud of our library and its 35,000 volumes. As I looked at the many different language volumes and newspapers, I had to scoff at the nerve of the miners saying that we don't care enough about them.

After I returned from the library last night, I found Father, Mr. Whitford and a sobbing Marian in our parlor. Father sternly summoned me to join the discussion. He told me that Marian was indeed pregnant, not with Lt. Col. Shotwell's child but with mine. I furiously denied ever having sexual relations with Marian. I told them that I had seen for myself Marian in compromising situations with the lieutenant. Mr. Whitford told me that Marian said that I forced myself on her the night that I walked her home after our trip to Electric Park. I admitted to being drunk but denied doing such an act. Marian never spoke or even looked me in the eye. Father dismissed the Whitfords and told them that I would do the honorable thing. Father wouldn't hear my excuses. He had already telegrammed Mother to return home for a wedding. Father would not hear my pleadings and declarations of love for Aili. Father's fury showed as he said, "For Gods sake, son! What's worse? You marrying for wealth and beauty or lowering yourself to the class of a Red Finn?"

After our meeting with the Whitfords's last night, I ran straight to Clara's boardinghouse. I was frantic as I told Aili and Clara about Marian's accusations. Aili ran off in tears at the news and Clara made me a stiff drink to calm my nerves. She counseled me to the best of her ability. She believed me, but felt that for Aili's benefit that I should not try to see or speak with her until I can prove my innocence. I left Clara's feeling suicidal. How can I live with Marian the rest of my life? How can I live with someone who has no shame at ruining the lives of others? I made my way home and planned to pack for a departure–hopefully with Aili, but father had already read my thoughts and was waiting for me in my bedroom. To entice me not to throw my life away, he's offered me his position at C & H upon his retirement in January. His retirement announcement was news to me and I'm sure something he considered only because of my current situation. He claims that he needs me because his health isn't what it should be. His words are pure gibberish, to keep me from Aili and on C & H's payroll. Doing the "right thing" for Marian was secondary to his wanting Marian's shares of C & H stock turned over to our family. He begged me to consider his offer.

When I awoke today, I still could not believe the predicament that Marian has placed me in. How could she lie about the true father of her child? I wanted to talk with Lt. Col. Shotwell, but he wasn't expected back to the region for several weeks, if at all. He surely wouldn't let an innocent man take the rap for his mistake. I yearn for Aili, but for her sake, I must stay away. I promised her that I'd never make her doubt my love. Surely, she must be heartbroken by my broken promise. If I refuse to marry Marian, then I'll be cut off from Father. Without a college diploma, I'll never be able to support myself as I'm accustomed, let alone support a family. I will have to tell Father that I'll go along with his plan but will plead with him to believe my story of innocence. I can only hope that the truth will reveal itself before Marian's pregnancy begins to show. The owners of C & H, with persuasion from Father, have agreed to meet with some strikers, non-WFM strikers, to try to resolve the strike. God damn this horrid business!

Father and I met Mother at the depot this morning. She cried when she saw me. I told her that it wasn't my child and she cried all the more. After returning Mother home, Father and I headed back to the office to wait for news from Governor Ferris. At the shaft closest to our office some 75 women again attacked the guards with broomsticks dipped in human excrement. The militia had to gain control of the mass by using horses to force them off the street. Father telegrammed General Abby's headquarters demanding that he declare marital law in the region. By evening we received word back that Governor Ferris refused General Abby's request. The Whitfords were at dinner tonight. It was disastrous. I felt like a commodity being auctioned off to the highest bidder. I glared at Marian the entire dinner. Twice tearfully she had to excuse herself from the table. She's trying to act so innocent and delicate. Father, however, was pleased with the dinner meeting. Mr. Whitford agreed to turn over more than 4 percent of the company's stock, Marian's shares, to me in accordance with Father's master plan.

I went to Aili's mother's grave today at our usual time. I had to see Aili. No matter what I'm being forced to do with Marian, I have to make sure that Aili believes that I haven't betrayed her love. She wasn't there, but she had been there because she left me a note and her agate. The note read:

> My Dearest,
>   Clara explained to me your predicament and your steadfast declarations of innocence. I want you to know that I do believe you because I could never believe that you would jeopardize a love as strong as ours. I do, however, believe that our lives were not meant to be shared. God does things according to His will and for some reason He does not see our lives as one united. I pray that you will be the perfect husband to Marian, and I feel that you will naturally be a wonderful father to Marian's child. It is in the child's best interest, that you should go along with the plans being made. You will prosper no matter your position.
> I'll be loving you,
Aili

I wept on her mother's grave and prayed to God that He should watch over the angel that he had blessed me with for a short time. I'm such a coward!

It was odd seeing the working miners being escorted to work and protected by their wives. The womens' resolve has been undeniable. The mine owners have appealed to Governor Ferris' decision against martial law. Judge Murphy will hear the appeal tomorrow. Marian had the nerve to come to my office today to see if I wanted to have lunch with her in the park. I told her that she surely must be mad and that any plans for her wedding should be arranged through Mother. At my response she immediately fell into a fit of sobs. Father heard the commotion in his office and was quick to calm Marian as he escorted her across the street to her office at the hospital. Father returned to my office in a rage and demanded that I immediately begin to play the game. As he left in a huff, he threw on my desk my newly acquired C & H stock certificates. Their worth is astonishing. Never did I dream that at such a young age I'd acquire so much wealth. The dividends alone are more than I ever dreamed of making on my own. By the end of the working day, I had apologized to Marian.

Father was quite pleased by my sudden change of face regarding Marian. "Now that's my boy!" he cried when I told him that I had come to terms with my new position in life. Sheriff Cruse came to the office today to tell us about some of the latest aggressive actions occurring in the region. We all laughed at the story of Mrs. William Teddy. It seems that she and her son-in-law were driving to console her son, who had recently lost both of his sons to mining accidents within the past two days. While enroute, a mob of strikers mistook them for scabs on their way to work and brandished them with sticks and rocks. One striker grasped the bridle and prevented the vehicle from proceeding any further. The horse became frightened by the commotion and threw Mrs. Teddy from the wagon. Because the strikers could not understand English, they could not understand her explanation of her mission. "They will eventually cannibalize themselves," chuckled Father. In retaliation for the owners appeal for martial law, the WFM group presented an appeal to the injunction to prevent the owners from hiring the men from Waddell-Mahon. We have a general feeling of confidence that the strikers will be worn down within a comparatively short time.

Father had me take control of an incident that occurred on company ground today. He said, "There's no time like the present for you to take over some of my responsibilities." I was called to the Red Jacket lock-up by Sheriff Cruse. I could not believe my eyes when I got there. Over 300 women had taken over the facility in anger over the arrest of six women. The women were arrested for attacking Wilbert Kasineimi, a C & H contractor. He carried the fatal dinner pail and, like a red flag to a bull, became a magnet for the angry strikers. Led by Big Annie, six women roughed him up pretty good and paid particular attention to scratching his face. Civil and military officers took Big Annie and five other women into custody. An Italian male by the name of Goggin was also arrested on a charge of inciting the riot. Sheriff Cruse and I negotiated for the women to be released on their own recognizance to appear at a hearing set for September 19th. This was agreeable to the mob of women and they broke up at the news of the women's pending release. As she left the jail, Big Annie winked at me and said, "I hear ya sold out kid...and I had such high hopes for you."

Marian was pleased that I came to see her last night. She told me her story of our so–called "consummation", one that we both knew was a lie. I kept my tongue and assured her that I would do my best to satisfy the demands placed upon me. Father was furious that I negotiated to have the six women released from the lock-up. "They should rot in hell as far as I'm concerned!" shouted Father. I explained to Father that Claude Taylor of Grand Rapids, President of the Michigan Federation of Labor, had assured me that he would be seeking an interview with us today or tomorrow. His plan would eliminate the WFM but would provide that men shall have the right to organize into local unions not affiliated with the federation. Mr. Taylor will propose that an arbitration committee be composed of seven members. Three will be appointed by the mine companies, three by the strikers and the seventh member by himself. "I will not be satisfied until the WFM quits the district," lamented Father. "Don't come to me until you can assure me of that." Today is Mother and Fathers twenty-fifth wedding anniversary. Although we're having dinner out tonight in recognition of their milestone, they don't really seem too excited about celebrating. Perhaps they married for reasons other than love too.

Claude Taylor tried to obtain an audience with Father and me today. Father told me to ask our attorney to inform Mr. Taylor that no arbitration scheme would be considered, as there is nothing to arbitrate. Since Mr. Taylor failed to submit a plan of arbitration, the WFM will await a visit from John A. Moffit of the Federal Department of Labor to present a proposition. I escorted Marian to a production at the opera house. I dreaded going there since I'd likely run into Aili. During intermission, many of Father's friends came up to congratulate us on our upcoming wedding. Mr. and Mrs. Whitford even sprang for a bottle of champagne to toast to our future. Just as the cork popped from the bottle and as Mr. Whitford shouted to our happiness, Aili crossed the foyer and raced up to the second floor balcony. I ran after her, but she escaped to the script room before I could reach her. Outside her door, I pleaded for her forgiveness. Marian pulled me away from the door and back into my unpleasant reality.

Today Governor Ferris made a proposal in vain to Attorney Darrow of the WFM. He provided that the strikers return to work pending an official investigation by a commission to be named by the governor for the elimination of the recognition of the federation. Darrow returned here today to condemn the Governor's plan, still holding out for full arbitration. Sheriff Cruse reported to me that twenty-four arrests were made today in the Copper Country, sixteen of which were women. The most important arrest though was that of Yanco Terisich, a Croatian agitator. Terisich has been next in importance only to Moyer in organizing the strike. As for Marian, she was hysterical that I ruined her engagement celebration last night. I didn't make any points with my future in-laws either. I vowed to be stronger, but I told her that I could never forget my love for Aili and she would have to learn to live with that truth as I have with hers.

I left Aili a note at her mother's grave to explain my future plans with Marian. I once again told her how sorry I was for hurting her and that I wished the best for her and Clara. My tears bled the ink on the note as I wrote it and my heart ached madly for her. I returned her agate along with the letter. As I walked home, I was caught among 2,000 strikers enroute to a rally at the Palestra. AFL treasurer John Lennon and Charles Moyer were scheduled to speak. As I made my way through the crowd, I saw Big Annie's flag getting closer and closer to me. As I stepped on to the boardwalk, she attacked me with her flag. Just as I was about to hit a lady, a guardsman came upon us and slashed Annie's flag. Other strikers saw this and came to her defense.

Father was in a foul mood today largely because of what seems to be a sudden influx of AFL and WFM leaders. Father is determined not to let C & H fall to their demands. Other mine operators across the country are watching us in earnest. What happens here will likely happen across the country. Father had me telegram the mine owners in Boston to let them know about Governor Ferris' proposal. They agreed to meet with non-WFM strikers if need be to resolve the situation. Having the mines at only 25 percent capacity and without adequate help disturbed them enough to agree to a meeting if necessary. Hopefully Darrow, Father and I can resolve the situation without having the owners travel to Michigan especially since the weather has turned colder and winter is just upon us. Father chastised me about the opera house incident. I assured him that I've closed that chapter in my life and will put C & H and Marian at first hand. Blanche Whitford and mother have set a wedding date of December 6th.

The strikers were out today, taking advantage of the sunny fall day. Even though the temperature was only 55, they continued upon their regular route. The difference today was that they were nailing white crosses to street signs and on light poles to mark each place where Sheriff Cruse's deputies have killed someone. I met with Marian over lunch today. She would like to go to Copper Harbor this weekend to see the fall colors on Brockway Mountain Drive. Aili would have loved to go on such a trip. I tried to talk Marian out of the trip, but she was adamant that it would solidify our engagement. Father knows of the plan and has already made plans to cover for my absence at the office on Friday. Lord give me the strength to find a palatable life with this woman.

Today Father and I received reports from each mine captain. The strike has significantly lowered the number of available men to work underground. C & H and Quincy have agreed to import workers from New York until the strike ends. I put together an appeal for Houghton's Circuit Judge, Patrick O'Brien, to restrict the strikers' demonstrations. Clearly their attacks on willing miners have caused many to stay home or to join the strike force. Judge O'Brien agreed to review our request this weekend. The strikers will surely riot over the importation of workers. The Citizens' Alliance has agreed to help get workers back to work. They've agreed to cut off all credit to any striker. With less disposable income available and because of the co-ops being set up, the business owners want the end of the strike just as badly as we do. They want the strike resolved before the slow winter season is upon them.

Sheriff Cruse had reports today of a shooting at the Isle Royal mine. A striker or strike sympathizer, while on picket duty between shafts No. 4 and No. 5, shot Randolph Harvey of Company A. The bullet came from the woods, but no trace of the assailant was found. Sheriff Cruse issued orders for General Abby, still on leave but in contact with present leaders, requesting all militia men to stay close to their camps because of the likely attack against the strikebreakers. I saw Clara today outside the post office. She was pleasant to me yet assured me that Aili would be fine with more time. She told me that Aili has joined a women's auxillary group to help unite the various families of the strikers. She laughed as she told me that their first goal was to write a Christmas script for the childrens' Christmas play to be held at the Italian Hall. I shuddered as I thought of myself being a married man by then.

~ *The Italian Hall where Aili is preparing her Christmas party for the children.* ~

Thirty strikebreakers are expected to arrive tomorrow. If their use proves successful, then it is said others will be brought in to work. I placed another call to Judge O'Brien to see if he'll consider a temporary order against the demonstrations. Due to Lennon and Moyer's presence in the Keweenaw, the strikers have been somewhat reserved. It's almost more unnerving than seeing them active with parades. On Tuesday the miners' union in Butte, Montana has decided to levy an assessment of one day's pay in October upon every member of the organization to assist the Michigan copper miners. This, in addition to the $2 a month for each man levied by the WFM members, should help to confer the $40,000 per week needed to support the strikers in Keweenaw and Houghton counties. Luckily most of the Butte funds won't arrive until November. Perhaps by then the strike will be over, or the strikers will be dead from frostbite or starvation. The strike is in its ninth week.

Judge O'Brien issued an injunction against the strikers today. They will face contempt of court proceedings if they commit any overt action against the mining companies and their employees. This includes intimidation, picketing or molestation of working men. Judge O'Brien will consider any needed revisions to the earlier issued injunction later this month. The union is already clamoring for its right to picket. The first strikebreakers arrived at the Quincy Mine at 5:40 this morning. This injunction should surely help to keep the strikers quiet during their arrival. Marian and I are supposed to depart by train at 8 a.m. tomorrow. It's bitterly cold today with snow expected. I will try to convince Marian that travel is not advised, especially in her delicate condition.

I was lucky to make it back from Copper Harbor. Marian wouldn't hear of not going on the color tour, so by 10 a.m. we finally departed. It was late afternoon by the time we got to Brockway Mountain. The sky had turned dark and threatening by then, but the colors were still spectacular. The wind was so strong that Marian's bonnet blew right off her head into the canyon. We stayed at the mountain lodge, where the innkeeper told us that the barometer had dropped so severely that an early winter storm was possible. We dined according to the innkeeper's schedule, and between courses I had to listen to Marian babble on about our future. I was amazed that she could act as if nothing had happened and that I was expected to act excited about her caper. We kept separate rooms according to protocol, but she tried to kiss me goodnight before she slipped into her room. I stayed awake till the wee hours of the morning looking into the fire and thinking of Aili. By the time I went to bed, the snow had begun to fall. By morning blizzard conditions existed, so we could not leave by carriage, but only by train. The train had to clear the tracks on several occasions. I was furious that I wasn't available to help Father with the strikers who had become unruly after hearing John Walker, president of the Illinois Mine Workers, speak at the Palestra. Five strikers were arrested for attacking workers on mine property.

September 25, 1913

Another train of 33 miners and trammers arrived from the east today. This time, however, it wasn't without incident. John Nummivuori and G. William Toppari, business manager and solicitor for the *Tyomies*, the Finnish socialist paper, induced 14 men, with $50 each, to take a train back to New York. The publishers, after huddling the men in a private room, failed to pay the $50. One broke loose and found his way back to the Quincy Mine where officers were brought back to release the others. As Nummivuori was arrested, he yelled to Hutchinson, a waddie, "You should be in Sing Sing!" Toppari put up a fight for his partner, and after a chase, both were secured and placed under arrest. The imported men were taken back to Quincy. Since more trouble seemed to be imminent for Sheriff Cruse, I requested the return of General Abby.

Judge O'Brien ruled against the strikers today. It will be great to have the streets of Red Jacket clear from parades. The WFM leaders are already filing appeals stating that the strikers have the right to parade and demonstrate at will. The strikers retreated to their homes fearing contempt of court charges. Some twenty C & H strikers came to me wanting their jobs back. I hired them back with their promise that they'd turn in their union cards. General Abby will arrive within the week. With the new ruling, he's ordered all but 500 of the guardsmen to return home. With the inclement weather coming and because most of their tents were blown down during the Sunday storm, the guardsmen will now be housed inside company homes. I wonder if Lt. Col. Shotwell will accompany General Abby? I doubt if he even knows that Marian has claimed me as the father of her child. Now that the stock's been transferred, it's probably not even worth discussing with him. I will not tell Marian of his upcoming return to the range. I'd rather let it be a surprise.

Red Jacket was quiet as a millpond today. The injunction seems to be working. At a meeting of the Mohawk strikers a vote was taken to return to work. The whistle may also blow at Ahmeek for the first time since July 23rd. Father is pleased with this news and eager to have our response to Darrow's arbitration plan made public today. Hopefully it too will encourage more strikers to return to work. In the reply we remind the strikers that the strike was called for only one reason, to get recognition of the union. WFM leaders have never formally submitted the grievances that they say are important, like the shorter workday, more money and the elimination of the one-man drill. We will state that the eight-hour day was being considered before the strike, but that many of the men didn't want it because it would cut their monthly income. Further, the standardization of pay is not feasible because of the differences in position requirements. Finally the one-man drill is an economic necessity because of the lessening percentage of copper available. It is here to stay.

Last night Marian and I had dinner at her house. Halfway through her main course I mentioned that Lt. Col. Shotwell was expected to return to Red Jacket by week's end. Her fork shook as she asked me what I was planning to tell him about our arrangement. I told her that I wasn't sure how I was going to handle seeing her friend. She reminded me about the stock and all of the pending wedding plans. "You do what you feel is in the best interest of C & H," she said. She knows that I would be jeopardizing my relationship with Father if I turned my back on her at this juncture. After dinner we walked down Fifth Street and ran into a mob outside the drug store. They were upset because their credit has been cut off, as planned, by the Citizens' Alliance. Among the crowd I saw Clara. My heart ached knowing that she might not be able to support her boarders. She was cut off because she houses some striking miners. Marian and I turned around and headed back toward home. Before we could turn the corner, the mob sighted us and started to run in our direction. Luckily we hopped on a passing trolley before they could catch up with us. Marian was quite bothered by the incident.

Not all of the strikers were weakening due to the injunction. Over 2,000 rallied at the Palestra to hear John Lewis of the American Federation of Labor and John Walker, President of the United Mine Workers of Illinois. The speakers told the crowd that the injunction was a plank of both the Republican and Democratic parties. Republican because the influence of the corporations has been largely Republican. Democratic because it was issued by a Democratic judge. "Vote the Socialistic ticket in all future elections," they advised. The speakers also came with the news that the executive council of the American Federation of Labor has agreed to levy a small assessment on the more than two million members of the federation's affiliated organizations for the benefit of the Michigan miners. Moyer was also in Washington requesting senators to procure a congressional investigation of the copper miners' strike, charging that the peonage laws have been violated. Regardless of these current events, the first arrests under the injunction occurred today. Two Finnish agitators were charged with contempt of court and picketing.

Father was not pleased with the American Federation of Labor's nation-wide assessment. He's hoping that Judge O'Brien's injunction will hold against the WFM's appeal on Monday. Sheriff Cruse was attacked last night as he left the Arlington Hotel. He was struck on the face with an edged weapon, which sheared off a major portion of his nose. He is recovering at the Laurium Public Hospital. I put Mother, Marian and Blanche on a train this morning. They're headed for Chicago to purchase a wedding dress for Marian. As Marian boarded the train, Lt. Col. Shotwell exited. They caught each other's eyes but continued in their own intended direction. I stopped the lieutenant as he started to pass me. Marian watched us in horror as her train left the station. Lt. Col. Shotwell was nervous as he congratulated me on my upcoming marriage. I wanted to kill him at that instance, but I turned the other cheek. Capitalism, my true friend, remains my only source of strength.

Tomorrow's the big legal battle, the hearing of the motion of the WFM for the dissolution or amendment of the injunction issued earlier by Judge O'Brien. It will be heard by the judge in the courtroom of the Houghton County building at 9 o'clock sharp Monday morning. The motion makes a sweeping claim for the dissolution of the injunction, declaring that the judge had no jurisdiction to make such a decision. The amendments asked for, in the event of the failure to arrive at dissolution, are for the purpose of permitting parades and picketing. I will take a train to Houghton today so that I can be there first thing in the morning. I will leave as soon as I get things in order at the armory. Meeri Saari, a fourteen-year-old girl of Quincy, has apparently gone mad over the strike. Last night at 3 a.m. she was caught tearing down the remaining guardsmens' tents while they were still sleeping in them. She was committed to the juvenile detention building, pending a hearing before the judge on Monday. General Abby and I will secure company homes for the displaced guardsmen.

I'm still in shock over Judge O'Brien's decision to dissolve the injunction issued on September 20th. He wrote, "On September 20th a writ issued on the bill filed by the complainants, I now feel that it was too broad and sweeping. This court will protect the rights of men who want to work, but also will protect the strikers in the peaceable use of argument and persuasion to induce others to refrain from work for the purpose of strengthening the position of the strikers. They have the right to combine, confederate and parade under proper conditions. The economic strength of the employing classes is in the control of the plants and the right to employ or reject applicants for work. The strength of the strikers is in their number and their right to combine. This court cannot and will not aid in breaking the strike, but it will give protection to all who want to work." As a result of the action, I had General Abby make preparations tonight to handle the expected activities of the strikers. Picketing had already resumed in Red Jacket by the time my train had returned from Houghton. Father was home resting in the study when I arrived. He looked ghastly, pale and lethargic as he discussed Judge O'Brien's decision. As he rested his eyes, he asked me to enforce the eviction notices and bring in more strikebreakers.

It was a regular jubilee in the range today. The strikers were parading with the earliest shift, and the demonstrations didn't cease even after the last shift of workers disappeared below ground. Sheriff Hepting of Keweenaw County has pleaded with Governor Ferris to send back more troops, asserting that the strike situation is beyond local control. Governor Ferris, in turn, ordered General Abby to prepare the Calumet forces to move north to monitor the Keweenaw situation. The strikers are now determined to prevent all work at the mines and to have all mine guards removed from the district. Our general counsel appeared before the State Supreme Court this afternoon and asked for a writ o mandamus to compel Judge O'Brien to place in operation an order restraining strike picketing and intimidation. The court, we've been told, did not announce when a decision would be rendered. The first train of strike guards should arrive on Friday. I've gathered a list of all strikers renting company houses. Almost all are past due rent at least 2 months. Since the

30 day warning of the original notice have passed, eviction can be immediate. Clara's boardinghouse is included on the list. Though her rent is current, I'm not sure that I can stop authorities from shutting down her operation.

October 4, 1913

Sheriff Cruse, now back to work, helped me scan a list for aggressive Finnish socialists currently renting homes from C & H. Over 500 names were identified. These people will be evicted first. At least this will spare Clara, who's Irish, for the time being. The Croats will be next. Father wants to rid Red Jacket of all socialists. Sheriff Cruse reported back to me after he had made several evictions. He had to call in General Abby to help protect him from the rock throwing that he encountered. He reported that Big Annie was soon on sight, and she spit right into his face. She was immediately arrested. The wives and children are running like mice to relatives' homes, most also owned by the company. Some are running to their local parish until better plans can be made. As I walked to Tamarack Park after my workday was complete, I saw a group of mothers and children being counseled by Aili. She saw me and quickly hustled the group into Clara's boardinghouse. As I continued on my walk, I was attacked from behind and knocked to the ground. My assailant was Aili, and she screamed at me for hurting innocent children. "Cutting off their food supply wasn't enough for you! You had to go and take the roof from above their heads too. You bastard. How could I ever have fallen in love with a man as evil as you?"

October 5, 1913

Like Aili, the strikers were furious at the news of the evictions. The action has resulted in the departure from the range of many Lithuanians and Italians. The railroad depot was packed with people leaving the area for the Butte copper mines or the Pennsylvania coalmines. Some are altogether leaving the U.S. with plans to return to their homelands. While the outgoing movement continues, we are bringing in labor steadily. Included among the men arriving are cowboys, miners and harvest hands. With few exceptions, they take well to the work. They have no complaints about the wages or conditions in the mines. Seeing Aili yesterday still haunts me. She's right. I'm a shallow beast. How could I endanger the lives of innocent children? What have I become? What about my dreams and aspirations? What good are riches if you don't have someone beautiful to share them with? I must end this bloody strike; otherwise I will never be able to pursue my wants. Aili is obviously out of the question now. Marian returns on Saturday. I still can't imagine myself tied to her for life. It seems like a jail sentence. Perhaps that's just what it is and just what I deserve. Greed has a price.

October 6, 1913

The first strikebreaker train arrived at Houghton today. A mob of strikers pelted the train with rocks and shattered almost every window on the passenger car. General Abby's troops had to come to Houghton to secure the train in order to allow the strikebreakers protection until they reached their designated stops. Father and I are worried about the potential danger of Mother's train returning home. Since Father didn't feel well again this evening, I opted to escape to the theater. During intermission I went down to the dressing rooms to see if Aili was working. She was, but as she saw me approach, she quickly slammed the door in my face. I couldn't concentrate on the production, so I left to have a drink at Clara's bar. She too was angered by the recent evictions and would not serve me. Never have I felt so alone. I walked back home only to find Father in bed and already asleep. Since I wasn't tired, I picked up the paper to read the front-page headline, which read *"Aili Maki: Organizing parade of children."* May God bless her.

October 7, 1913

Sheriff Cruse found me at the office on Saturday to inform me that a train, carrying 42 employees from the Ascher Detective Agency from New York, was partially blown up this morning. Engineer Cocking saw a smoking fuse just ahead of his train as he was pulling into the Copper City Depot. He stopped the train one-train length ahead, but the dynamite explosion was strong enough to blow up a large section of rail, which caused the passenger train to derail on to its side. Sheriff Cruse informed me that Mother, Marian and Blanche were passengers on the train and that Mother and Blanche's bodies had been taken to the morgue, while Marian was at the hospital recovering from the loss of her unborn child. I was stunned and disoriented after he left. I promptly left to inform Father, who was at the house resting. By the time I arrived, he had already heard the news. Instead of mourning the loss of Mother, he was more concerned with what my intentions were to be regarding Marian. "I would encourage you to pursue the plans as already arranged. Marian awaits your visit at the hospital. I suggest that you go. I will make the necessary preparations regarding Mother's remains." I can't believe that he still expects me to marry Marian and that he could be so callous towards losing Mother.

October 8, 1913

Last night when I arrived at Marian's room at the hospital, Lt. Col. Shotwell was sitting on the edge of her bed. Marian was crying and clearly shaken by the loss of her child and her mother. I left the room and was later approached by the lieutenant. He apologized for not supporting Marian and for allowing me to take the blame for her pregnancy. He said that he and Marian have worked out arrangements to marry and that I'm no longer required to make such a sacrifice. I left the hospital stunned. At first I wanted to run to Aili to tell her the news. Finally I had proof that it hadn't been my child. First, however, Father needed me so I went back to the house to help him prepare for Mother's viewing. Father was once again angered when I told him about Marian and Lt. Col. Shotwell. "God damn it! We need that stock now more than ever!" he yelled. Then he broke down into a fit of sobs. The stress of the mine and mother's death has proven to be too much for him. He apologized to me for selling off my dreams for company stock. "I still refuse to allow you to chase that Finnish girl. You have assumed a leadership role at the company, and, by God, you will see this strike to the end."

Mother's funeral was today. After the viewing, we escorted her casket to her final resting place at the cemetery. Our procession was briefly interrupted by a parade crossing of more than 500 children. I had forgotten about the parade that Aili had staged. There she was, front and center, leading children carrying signs that read "PAPA IS STRIKING FOR US!" Father noticed Aili right away and glared at me as she passed. Aili looked at me with sympathy for the loss of my mother. At least she has a little heart left for me. Father's right. I cannot put Aili through this turmoil. I must see that this strike gets settled, and then I will be able to decide how I want to live the rest of my life. Mother's gravesite was near Aili's mother's grave. Perhaps I will see her on visiting days. Father and I went back to the house to be with relatives after the burial. Clara called on us, even though she's still angry about the evictions. She assured me that everything would work out in the long run. She also said that Aili now knows the truth about Marian but that she's still deeply troubled about the strike matters.

⁓ Aili's Childrens' Parade. ⁓

Truancy laws may be imposed upon the parents of the parading children. Aili once again led the children, dressed in their Sunday best, around the streets of Red Jacket and Laurium. Today the Michigan Supreme Court upheld the law of September 20th, once again prohibiting the acts of parading and picketing. The strikers responded violently, and aggressive plans for future violence are being made. More attacks on the Keweenaw Central trains are planned in opposition to the importation of guards and strikebreakers. The mines are making preparations to start production again now that some form of martial law is in place. With production only at one-half of normal, even less at other mines, the sounds of the pumps running will be a welcome sign. Aside from the children still parading, the range has been fairly quiet. At least with the children on strike, I can watch Aili from my office window. I've made a promise to myself not to see her until the strike is settled. Our emotions are just too volatile right now. Father still shows signs of stress and illness. I've been trying to do as much work as possible to lighten his load. He's been sleeping a lot. Perhaps it's just his way to mourn for Mother.

The quiet of yesterday was too much for the strikers. Sheriff Cruse tells me that a mob erupted at the Mohawk mine because the strikers tried to take control of the pumps and a deputy sheriff was shot and killed in the scuffle. The strikers claim that it was a guard's gun that killed the sheriff. The guards claim that it was a gun from a striker. Sheriff Cruse will lead an investigation. The children paraded again today. Starting Friday, truancy laws will be imposed upon parents. If Aili doesn't comply with the laws, she may end up in jail herself. More evictions occurred today. Many are scrambling to get their jobs back at the mine. If there is history of strike violence or if they refuse to turn in their WFM membership cards, then they don't get rehired. If they're Finnish, they don't get rehired at all. Never before was nationality an issue. Now each miner is categorized by nationality, membership and past work history. Several arrests have been made under the new injunction. With the cold weather, evictions and injunctions, workers are flocking back to their old jobs. Sometimes they beg for leniency.

Today Sheriff Cruse arrested scores of parents under the truancy law. He called me down to the jail to see the circus that was occurring. Hundreds of parents were behind bars, and hundreds of children were outside the cells crying. Judge O'Brien called for their immediate release but scheduled hearings for them in November. One instigator, Aili, however, was not given leniency. She looked like a wounded bird in a cage but still acted defiant and headstrong as I approached her cell. "Aili!" I cried. "What have you done to yourself?" "It's for the children, Eston. Don't you see? Look around you. The children are frightened, hungry and alone. You've taken so much from them and for what?" she declared. The sight was pathetic. Aili was right. This strike has done more harm than good. I told Aili that I couldn't help matters until the WFM pulls out of the district. As I left the jail, Aili screamed, "You don't understand, Eston! You don't know what's real!"

I fronted Aili the bail money anonymously. I was told that she refused to leave until she posted her own bond because she wouldn't take "blood money." Clara arrived with the bail, and Aili was released with a hearing date set for November. Marian came to see me at my office today. She cried as she apologized for what she had done to me. She and Lt. Col. Shotwell will wed and leave the region as soon as the strike is over. She wished me luck with Aili. "You seem to love her very much," she said. I declined comment and she left with her stock certificates. Father returned to work today. His pallor still seems ashen. He officially changed my title to Assistant Mine Captain. I will also see a significant raise and stock assignments. He had me gather names of all Finnish farmers operating on company-leased land. I'm sure that evictions will soon follow. In celebration of my raise, I went to the theater. I missed having my mother's company. I could only imagine what Aili was doing down below in the dressing chambers. It seems like years ago that we enjoyed loving moments there. Before I knew it, the show had ended, and I found myself walking home in the cold rain.

The Fifth Street stores were the targets of the strikers today. The strikers, fed up with having to pay cash, stoned all of the stores which had recently revoked credit honors to the strikers. The strikers went on to stone the windows of the merchants' homes. Sheriff Cruse arrested as many as possible but without the help of General Abby and his men. They were in Mohawk helping with the riots there. As a result, eviction notices were issued to all Finnish farmers leasing company land. This will cut off the miners' food supply, and the strikers will be at the mercy of WFM supplies, which have been scarce. No longer will the red socialists be able to contribute farm products to the strikers or assist strike agitators. Over 500 farm leases will be cancelled within thirty days. Since most of the farmers aren't current or profitable anyway, the land could be put to better use. The lease arrangements were truly just another thing that C & H did to help the miners have additional income from the range. Father also issued eviction notices to all remaining non-workers. This includes Clara's boardinghouse. I will have to issue the notice to her personally.

I brought flowers to Mother's grave today with hopes of seeing Aili. She was there, but she started to run away when she saw me approach. I grabbed her before she could go and forced her to look at me and tell me that she doesn't love me anymore. She spit in my face as she said, "I despise you!" As she ran away, I yelled, "Don't come crying to me when you get evicted!" On my way home I stopped at Clara's and nailed the eviction notice on the front door. Aili came to the door and tore off the notice and threw it at my feet. As I walked away, I was plummeted with rotten tomatoes. When I got home, Father laughed at the sight of me. "It's lonely at the top, isn't it, son?" he cried. I asked him where all of the evictees will go. Unable to answer, he left the room laughing. Furious, I went upstairs to bathe. I had to laugh myself at the absurdity of it all. After my bath, Father and I went to the club. We had a wonderful time. For some reason, we were able to forget the strike. We drank, laughed and even cried over the recent events. Father and I stumbled home only to find several dozen miners and their families camped out on our front lawn. Father looked at me and said, "I guess that answers your earlier question, son!"

It took Sheriff Cruse four hours to clear our yard of the striking miners and their families. Some of the ethnic organizations are offering to house the families. Another situation occurred today that has intensified feelings in the strike zone. Joseph Manerich, a striker from Centennial, had a scuffle with Deputy Sheriff Pollack. The incident left both dead. At the strikers meeting today, the speakers censured the authorities for alleged negligence in investigating the aforementioned situation. Obviously the writ reissued by the Michigan Supreme Court last Wednesday seems to be failing because picketing is still happening on a regular basis on the range. Arrests can only be made if the picketing, which is permitted if done constructively, becomes intimidation. The strikers want the arrest of Sheriff Cruse for allowing deputies to carry guns. Due to the blanket license, which allows for guns on mine property, Sheriff Cruse defends any deputy carrying an arm to protect the working strikers and the company property. Sheriff Cruse has requested a leave of absence until the strike is settled. He and his wife will leave the range for relatives near Lansing as soon as the Under Sheriff, Carl Nelson, takes over as interim-Sheriff.

In response to the two recent killings, tempers flared between the strikers and deputies. According to eyewitnesses, a passing automobile fired directly into a marching mob of men, women and children. Although passing bullets grazed a few, it's reported that no one was seriously injured. Major Britton's Signal Corps were able to stop the sniper's car. It's believed that the men were drunk and employees of the Ascher Detective Agency. Sheriff Cruse and I met with Under Sheriff Nelson to discuss security proceedings. It's clear that the strike has taken its toll on Sheriff Cruse. Not only is he visibly disfigured from the strike, but he also appears to be a bundle of nerves. He says that he will return to the range after the strike. His reputation has been damaged because clearly he hasn't had good control since the strike began. Rock shipments are up slightly this week. The working forces have increased due to the return of the Cornish workers, who had left for Iron County at the start of the strike. Many Italians plan to return to work tomorrow morning.

Clara stopped by the house today to inform me that she is able to pay ahead in rent at the boardinghouse if that will keep the evictors away. She also told me that Aili was injured at the Centennial parade yesterday and that she's at the C & H hospital recuperating. After Clara left, I immediately went to the hospital to check on Aili. She looked tired. Perhaps she was too tired, because she allowed me to sit next to her. For a long time we both just sat there with no words exchanged. Finally, I told Aili how sorry I was that the strike has caused so much pain for her and many innocent people. I explained the company's position. As I spoke, she turned her head and looked blankly out the hospital window. After I finished, she asked me, "What's important to you, Eston?" I was tongue-tied. Everything that I tried to say came out as, "The Company feels…" or "Father says…" Clearly she had made her point. I was not living for myself, but for others. "Isn't it time for you to listen to the people? C & H has been a good parent for years, but the mines have outgrown their methods. The world has changed. It's time to listen to the people." A lone tear fell from her eye as she listened to me promise her that I'd try to compromise on some of the strikers' demands.

Today is Aili's eighteenth birthday. I went to the hospital to help her check out, but she had already been discharged. I then went to Clara's to see if I could find her there. Clara told me that she was in Laurium at a morning demonstration. I found her marching proudly with her grazed arm in a sling! I pulled Aili from the crowd and made her come with me to a destination unknown to her. She was wild with excitement and touched that I had remembered her birthday. I brought her to the children's park where I presented her with a birch tree sapling. We eagerly planted the young tree and christened it with fresh water. As we stood in front of our tree, Aili reached for my hand. We both cried as we cherished the tree and our intimate moment together. For us, the tree represented a rebirth of our love. After our special moment had passed, I insisted on taking Aili home so that she could get some much needed rest. When I returned to the office, Father summoned me to his office. "While you were out fraternizing with your socialist Finn, an explosion occurred at shaft No. 3 and possibly more than 70 miners are dead. You must go now to pacify the crowds. Cries of negligence have already been heard!"

October 20, 1913

I arrived to the shaft just one hour after the fire was discovered. The mine captain explained to me that the fire had started in the twenty-seventh level and that he had tried to get a hose connected to the pump at that level, but the smoke had already filled No. 3 and No. 4. He had tried to send men down No. 1, 2 and 5 in order to warn others to leave immediately. While some of the miners fought the fire, another shift sat down for lunch, not fearing that the fire would spread vertically or horizontally. Their assumptions were wrong. Reversing the normal flow of air, the smoke and gas went back into the mine. I was faced with the decision to cap the shafts to control the fire and kill any that remained alive down below or keep the shafts open to allow for any escapes. Assuming most were already dead, I opted to keep the shafts open until 5 p.m., at which time I only would shut down No. 3. I had the mine captain organize a search team for tomorrow. By the time I returned back to the office, I had to face the wrath of the families of the missing men.

October 21, 1913

The search teams recovered one captain, 19 miners, 5 trammers and 4 young boys. The fire had burned from the twenty-seventh level to the sixth level. A coroner's hearing is set for one week from yesterday to determine fault. Due to the fire, Father and I decided not to enforce the eviction notices any further. Many of the strikers have already moved, no longer wanting company aid. After Father and I met our work obligations, I wanted to see Aili. Knowing that she would blame Father and me for the fire, I gave my plans a second thought. Instead I went to the club for dinner and spirits. General Abby, Under Sheriff Nelson and Lt. Col. Shotwell offered me a seat at their table. Liquor was the only thing that seemed to take my mind off the recent mine deaths. It didn't, however, let me forget Aili. My heart ached for her and the more I looked across at Lt. Col. Shotwell, the angrier I got that he had almost ruined my life. Before I knew what I was doing, I got up to leave, but not before I punched the lieutenant squarely in the nose.

By the time I awoke on Sunday, Father had already heard about my incident with Lt. Col. Shotwell. He threatened to send me back to Boston to resume my studies if I didn't immediately assume the role of corporate leader. In my mind that wasn't a threat. Aside from the money and Aili, I wouldn't miss anything on the range. He assigned over Mother's shares of stock to ensure that I had an even more vested interest in seeing C & H resume mining capabilities to its fullest potential. He used our Superior facility, south of Houghton, as an example of fine leadership. That region was expected to be the worst in regards to picketing and violence. However, due to Potter's fine engineering efficiencies, he was able to show how the one-man drill could be used successfully. Considering that this piece of machinery is one of the miners' biggest grievances, it's a true accomplishment. In fact, the Superior is expected to be at full capacity by Monday. The strike zone in Red jacket was calm today despite the recent mine explosion. A meeting did occur at the Palestra, but the speakers offered no new information to the lessening number of listeners. Aili was not at her mother's grave when I stopped to visit Mother's grave. Now that my stake in C & H is more significant, perhaps I should limit my visits with Aili.

A great blizzard raged today. Since I was in conference with our attorneys all day, the storm didn't hamper my activities. They're preparing our statements in regard to how we handled the explosion. By nightfall the roads were impassable, and the walk home was daunting. Under Sheriff Nelson arrived to inform us that a fire was raging at the boardinghouse of Thomas James of Centennial Heights. The fire was discovered by a neighbor girl around 6 o'clock, whereupon a hundred or more strikers appeared out of nowhere to jeer and hoot at the building. It's believed that the fire was set by strikers in opposition of James' housing of some 30 to 40 Ascher detectives employed at the Centennial Mining Company. They were all out on guard duty at the time of the fire, so no bodily injuries occurred. We telegraphed Governor Ferris about the most recent incident, hoping that some of the National Guardsmen could return to the region. After Under Sheriff Nelson left, Father and I continued to discuss our strike strategy. Tomorrow he wants me to review the farm leases in detail and begin to force evictions.

Today both Houghton and Calumet were overcome with clashes. In Houghton one hundred or so Italian strikers attacked a Northwestern train that arrived from the east. Assuming that the passenger train contained scabs, they tried to disconnect the train from the baggage car. They succeeded. The baggage car worked itself away from the station and tipped off the tracks as it ran into the southbound train. The strikers continued to pellet the passenger car with snowballs. Several of the strikers even fired revolvers. Also in Houghton, hundreds of Finnish servant girls went on strike to protest our recent announcement of the cancellation of farm leases. In Red Jacket during a melee on Portland Street, Under Sheriff Nelson received a bad knife wound in his shoulder and head. The injuries required surgical attention. The deputies had to use their riot sticks to push back the crowds. It was then that the under sheriff received his injuries. He was not prepared for the large number of knives and blackjacks that were present at the fray. The scores of men arrested in the incident are being accused of posting bond property not belonging to them but to other strikers. We are contemplating charges of perjury.

Today I finally got to see Aili. As I suspected, she was not happy with the continued deaths occurring on the range. She was even armed with a Houghton County mine inspector's report which showed that 54 of 1,000 workers were likely to be killed in the mines, a number much larger than other mining communities like those in California or Montana. Regardless of the continued tension regarding the company, we were still happy to see each other. Although the weather was still brisk and the recent snowfall made our walk a struggle, we walked to the livery yard, which was being flooded for Red Jacket's outside skating rink. We watched as the men prepared the rink. We were both excited at the prospect of skating. I promised to take Aili skating when the rink was ready. Aili looked beautiful. The cold had made her cheeks rosy, and the bitter air made her eyes slightly watery, only enhancing their blueness. We went back to Clara's for tea and warmth and discussed everything but C & H.

Father was angered by my mysterious disappearance yesterday. I assured him that I had been at the Oceola Mine clarifying the recent events. Today our attorney issued a statement that C & H was not at fault in the tragedy. They continued to state that the men killed in the mine had had ample warning to remove themselves from the danger zone. However, they had made some incorrect assumptions and opted to remain in the mine. We had several grieving widows at the office today threatening lawsuits. We referred them to our attorneys. Father did not want to make a settlement because then it would appear that we had been at fault, and with the current strike situation, it would only give the WFM more ammunition against us. We also had a report that a train leaving Hancock for Calumet was fired upon. Over 70 shots were fired as it climbed the Sweedetown hill. In addition to the two carloads of imported workers, it also was carrying mail, baggage and regular citizens. We immediately made plans to visit the governor in Lansing to discuss the continued attacks. Post Office special agents will also arrive to investigate the attacks on the mail trains. We will be asking Judge O'Brien to add more restrictions to his most recent writ.

Father, our attorneys and I traveled to Crystal Falls to see Judge O'Brien. We pleaded for greater protection from the strikers. Mother's death on the rails was just one of the many reasons to cause the judge to issue a blanket writ of attachment, which permitted the arrest at sight of violators of the injunction against the WFM. In protest, some WFM leaders were already at Governor Ferris' office in Lansing pleading the new writ as unconstitutional. The writ is the first of its kind stating that an entire group of demonstrators can be arrested on sight whether or not they were the key instigators. We also met with General Abby to request that Sheriff Cruse be asked to help out once again with the strike. With Under Sheriff Nelson recuperating, Cruse's expertise and knowledge of the mine properties are inherent to our success. Lt. Col. Shotwell and I are getting along fine now that the score has been settled. Marian is recuperating nicely and eager for the strike to end so that she can marry and repair her reputation.

The first arrests of the blanket writ happened today when 141 strikers were arrested at the Allouez Street railway station. Shortly thereafter another 85 were delivered by rail car. The 226 men were arrested under contempt charges. Judge O'Brien issued a lengthy statement pleading the strikers to seek peaceful solutions. It read, "It is better to lose the strike than to lose your reputation for being law abiding citizens." If the writ continues to be upheld in this manner, then we feel that the strike's end is near. While he slept at Sheriff Cruse's house, the under sheriff awoke hearing a noise outside the house. Being sure that the strikers were on the attack, he fired several shots toward the noise. It was Goose, Sheriff Cruse's dog. Father chuckled at the news of the dog's demise. He never did like the mutt. It was good to see Father involved again. He's looking better, but there still seems some level of detachment about him. Perhaps it's just the loss of Mother that's bothering him. Then again, it could just be this horrid strike business. At the news of the latest train incident, the owners from Boston informed us of their scheduled arrival next week.

All trains arriving in the Copper Country must now be accompanied by large military detachments. The scabs were warned ahead of time that they may be shot at. The workers arriving now from Detroit, Chicago and New York all feel that the wages and conditions warrant the risk. General Abby is doing his best job, but he has called in the U.S. Marshals to investigate the rail troubles. The Department of Justice, the U.S. Post Office and the Railway Service will take over the prosecution of the seven men arrested for the shooting at the Northwestern train last week. Until the rails become more secure, automobile trucks will chauffeur the mail. I met Aili at the theater. No production was in town, but she was repairing costumes from the last production. As she mended, we discussed the strike and how the end must be near. We talked about our dreams and freedoms that we would share once it was over. Father would remain our sole obstacle once the strike ended. I joked that maybe he and Clara could become friendly. Aili really found humor in my statement.

Although the mines were closed today, the crowds were unruly. The miners met at the Italian Hall today, and speakers urged more aggressive tactics. Large demonstrations of picketing and parading occurred after the rally. Father and I could hear the strikers from our church pew. We felt very uncomfortable as we prayed before some of the other parishioners, mostly strikers. After church Father reddened as he said, "By God, we built this church! I can pray in it!" We visited Mother's grave after church. Aili as usual was there. Much to my surprise, she came up to Father and offered her condolences. He was taken aback but seemed to admire her nerve. With a twinkle in his eye, he said, "Such a pretty girl...but a Finn!" We worked the rest of the day preparing our statements on the strike for our month end conference with the mine owners.

After hearing our report, the mine owners want us to meet with an intermediary. Due to the number of dead and arrested, they thought that it was in our best interest to resolve the issue of WFM recognition immediately. In reaction to the U.S. Marshal and Postal Service investigation, mail chauffeurs went out on strike too. The police and secret service were called upon to guard the wagons as other men tried to deliver the mail. Sheriff Cruse is expected back to the district by tomorrow. Judge O'Brien gave the strikers a victory today by postponing the prosecution of those recently arrested en mass. He ordered the sheriff to release without bail any person arrested and scheduled them to appear at hearings later. The Allouez demonstrators won't go to a formal hearing until early December. Father and I stormed Judge O'Brien's chamber to lambaste him for his erratic rulings. The ruling will stand, but the strikers will not have serious repercussions for not abiding by the ruling.

It's reported that Guy Miller, executive board member of the WFM, pulled out of the district permanently. Some WFM socialists openly blame Guy Miller for precipitating the strike with promises of relief funds. Continued criticism from the socialist strikers and rifts between him and Moyer may also have led to his desertion. All in all, it was great news for the mine owners. Another sign that the strike's end is near was disclosed in the Finnish daily paper, *The Paivalehti*. One striker was quoted as saying, "The fact is that the majority of the Finns were strongly against the strike, but a lot of us have been forced by the local and outside socialists and union agitators to join the union…we are not getting enough from the union to keep things up with our families." The article continues to plead for the strikers to return to work. I went to the newsstand to get a copy of the paper and quickly delivered the news to Aili and Clara. Neither was home, so I left a note with the article for them to read. They will be pleased by today's changes.

Sheriff Cruse was shocked to find his house doused with kerosene this morning. Apparently news of his return had spread to the strikers. I pity any striker who might cross his path any time soon. He is determined to end this strike even if it means putting every striker in jail. He learned about Goose when visiting the under sheriff at the hospital. I finally caught up with Aili at the schoolyard today. She was pleased with the news of Miller's pullout and the news in the article that I had left them to read. "So what will you be conceding to?" she asked. "Surely just because the WFM may pull out doesn't mean that the strikers will continue on in the manner before the strike started." I asked "Why not? We gave them everything. Look around. Are things so bad?" These were the wrong words to say to Aili. She left angry with me, and I made no attempt to follow her.

A heavy snowfall in Red Jacket today has seemed to have an effect. The strikers at the Wolverine Mine are rumored to want to return to work. C & H shipped 7,600 tons of rock today, just 200 short of normal. We've offered to re-employ, regardless of nationality, those of the striking miners and trammers who will give up their membership in the WFM and who haven't been identified with any strike violence. The Finnish businessmen continue to advise the Finnish strikers, 50 percent of whom make up the striking population, to return to work. I watched Aili at the yard rink today. I threw a snowball at her as she twirled around the rink. She pretended not to notice me.

At Quincy today a young miner's son pulled off quite the prank. He spied an empty telephone cable spool on the street. He released a block of wood that held the spool from rolling down the street. The 1000-pound spool gained speeds of 30 miles per hour as it rolled down the main hill in Quincy. It came to a halt by hitting a water plug. The water flooded businesses and quickly froze the streets. Cars became snarled, and it took hours for the police, fire and water departments to restore order. William MacDonald, Michigan's State Representative, briefed President Wilson on the Michigan strike situation today. MacDonald pleaded for executive action or legislation to improve the conditions at the mines in order to preserve the posterity of an immense industry. The President said that he would look into the situation and was regretful that the federal mediation board did not have the power to take on the strike matter. We're making preparations to house replacement workers. Boardinghouses are being built since many of the miners who were given eviction notices still remain in the company owned homes. John Walker will again address a mass meeting of copper strikers here on Sunday. It seems that the WFM just won't let go. It's time that they admit to defeat.

Judge O'Brien summoned Father and me to his chambers for a private meeting today. He claims that the WFM will wave the white flag if we agree to take the miners back without making them leave the union. "Absolutely not!" yelled Father. "We've come this far, and we will not recognize the WFM or its members in any way, shape or form." After our meeting with the judge, we continued to discuss our plans. If we continue to issue eviction notices and make plans to replace all union workers, then the strikers should see that the union promises are false and that the mines can operate and will operate without their presence. If what Judge O'Brien says is true, then the strikers should be flocking back in groves. I have taken the stance to remain separated from Aili until the strike ends, which should be within a few days. We will probably consider better arbitration methods and shorter workdays after the strike. If we give in now to those demands, it will just fuel the strikers to want more later on.

John Walker has given the strikers strong assurance that they will be taken care of financially. He has plans to attend the convention of the American Federation of Labor in Seattle. He will urge additional support for the Michigan copper district. He also plans on visiting the Butte district to ask for additional strike benefits. Many of the strikers walked out on his speech, just another sign that many of the strikers are becoming discontented with false promises. Many have not forgotten that Walker once promised, "...no one would suffer hunger or cold or nakedness." The federation spellbinders and agitators seem to be making last ditch efforts to gather piecemeal donations. It's rumored that the federation has spent most of its funds supporting efforts of the likes of Moyer and Miller. Finnish leaders have advised the strikers to abandon mass picketing and rallies in response to some recent mine deaths. They're also trying to induce them to leave the union and return to work. Only a small number of federation men, however, have returned to work.

The clamor for aid from the federation for the strikers seems to be bearing fruit. Three cars of coal for thousands of strikers were reported to have arrived today. Three cars of meat are also expected to arrive. The Hennessy chain of cost stores under WFM auspices has been proposed. The cost stores may cause further hard feelings between the strikers and business owners. Thus far the owners have yielded to all nationalities. Most have reextended credit and honored the federation's strike benefit order for goods. The new stores promise to take business away from these merchants. It's rumored that the Citizens' Alliance group is planning to reorganize in response to this news. Our company, as well as others, is continuing on with our efforts to import workers and expand production. Fifty Greek miners and trammers were brought in for work. No attacks other than verbal occurred at the field as they arrived.

Last night we met with the sheriff and Governor Ferris' latest representative. It's likely that the governor will not remove the remaining guardsmen due to the prospect of violence that may occur against the imported workers. The sheriff has finally moved back to his home after its recent dousing. He has been keeping busy with the rash of mass arrests. Because of Judge O'Brien's leniency of late, the strikers don't fear being arrested. The court dockets are packed with upcoming hearings of those arrested and released. Two Hennessy cost stores have opened today, one at Ahmeek and one in Copper City. Three carloads of provisions are expected to stock the stores tomorrow. I was approached by John Black, a director of the Citizens' Alliance, to help finance the publication of *Truth*, their publication. In the document the alliance will outline their beliefs and efforts to rid the copper fields of the WFM. Several mine owners have agreed to finance the club's efforts, but anonymously.

The Citizens' Alliance group, with large corporate backing, rapidly has become a large force in opposition to the WFM. Members espouse that the union's poisonous propaganda of destructive socialism, violence, intimidation and disregard of law and order must come to an end. They chanted that the WFM is a "menace to the future of the Copper Country" as they organized at their first rally today. It's unsure who started the group, but it's made up of merchants, bankers and regular citizens who want the WFM out of the Keweenaw as much as the mine owners do. Over 20,000 members were at a rally, and all were given a button to wear to proclaim their allegiance. In opposition to the new group, the miners got hold of some of the buttons and paraded with them fastened to the seats of their pants. Sheriff Cruse's deputies were shot at as they tried to break up the demonstration. By evening, the weather had turned dismal, so Father and I went home to make our own dinner. When we served eviction notices on the Finnish farmers, Mamie, our Finnish servant, quit her duties and joined the strike force. Tonight we both missed Mother and the way things used to be. A warm smile from Mother would have been very welcoming on such a cold and blustery night.

The cold winds continued today, but it wasn't cold enough to deter the miners or the alliance members from demonstrating. One band of Citizens' Alliance members raided homes of the strikers and confiscated all weapons found on the premises. Luckily the weather had turned stormy after the raids, so the strikers didn't come out in force to oppose the alliance group. Father and I once again retreated to our home to wait out what looked like a very bad storm. We both retired to our own rooms to be alone with our own thoughts. I thought that I'd write to Aili but then decided against it. She will see that we care for the strikers, just not the WFM, when we institute shorter hours and grievance sessions for miners. That should appease her, and by then the strike should be near its end. It's unbelievable that the strike has been going on for almost four months now. I'm sure that the WFM had no idea that it would continue on in such a manner. Giving up here would surely end the WFM nationwide. Hanging on is only for principle now. Unfortunately Moyer's stubbornness has caused great hardships. We are different than the rest of the nation's mines. We've done a lot for Red Jacket and will continue to do so once the union leaves the district.

By morning, almost three feet of snow had fallen. By noon the trucks and rollers had cleared a path down Fifth Street, but most of the other roads still remain closed. In spite of the snow, several hundred strikers still managed to parade down Fifth Street. After Sheriff Cruse and the mounted police worked to break up the crowd, 99 strikers were arrested and incarcerated at the jail. Since the armory jail has been dismantled, the regular jail was over capacity. By now over 400 arrests have been made against strikers violating the injunction. The Citizens' Alliance members attacked some of the strikers as they were released on their own recognizance. There was little movement the rest of the day, largely due to the ever-increasing amount of snow falling. I snowshoed to the library to get a book to read. When I arrived, a sign was posted stating that it was closed due to the storm. From the library I decided to walk down Fifth Street in hopes of finding at least a current newspaper to read. As I turned a corner, I could see a line of people, mostly women and children, lined up at the newest cost store. The mothers were doing their best to keep the children warm against the howling wind. Many of the children only had rags wrapped around their hands for warmth.

The snow still continues to fall. Father and I felt stifled being unable to even make it to the office. We played chess in front of the fire until he became weary of the match and opted for a nap instead. Bored and unable to sit one moment longer, I decided to snowshoe over to Clara's boardinghouse. I didn't care if they were mad at me; I had to get out of the house. At the very least, I could tell them that we were considering a shorter workday and a method to hear grievances. Aili answered the door and was quite shocked to find me standing there. I told her about our plans at the mine, and, as I thought, it was enough to gain entrance. As she hugged me, she said, "I'm glad that you're having a change of heart!" Clara was relieved with the news and treated me to freshly baked corn bread and tea. I've never felt more at home.

I never made it home last night. Within minutes of arriving at Clara's we were all having a wonderful time. The other tenants joined us around the fire, and the stories they told were endless and our greatest source of entertainment. By nightfall I couldn't see one foot in front of my face because the snowfall was so heavy. I figured that Father was going to be furious with me no matter what I did at this point, so I decided to stay the night at Clara's. Aili and I slept on mats before the fire. We held each other close the entire night. We both know the strength of our love but were hesitant to express our feelings because of our uncertain future. We have high hopes for our dreams but fear the reality of our present day.

As I expected, Father was furious that I hadn't returned the other night. He didn't even have to ask about my whereabouts; he knew. "You will be sent home to further your studies once the thaw comes. I suggest that you end your relations with Aili, for she will not be going with you." Going back to Boston used to be the thing I wanted most. Now it's secondary to being with Aili. I brought up the idea again of offering the strikers shorter workday and regularly scheduled grievance periods. He erupted again and spewed out, "God damn it, Eston. Don't you see what's happening? Anything that we give, they'll want more later. We will lose total control of our industry, our profits. Our current system has not only made us a healthy profit, but the dividends have also benefited Boston and Red Jacket. Both are wonderful communities, grown by our generosity. With the price of copper dropping and lodes depleting, we have to protect what we have. You must not give in to them, Eston. You must develop a backbone. That Aili has softened you. Don't be blinded by love!" As he rambled on, I could not erase the image of the cold and hungry children at the cost store. Perhaps we've outgrown paternalism.

Finally the snow ceased, and the sun was blinding after three days of dark skies. The road crews were working overtime trying to get the major thoroughfares cleared for traffic. Luckily the trolleys were running as well as the trains. Sheriff Cruse alerted us that the strikers had dynamite set off at the home of Alina Salminen. Alina's boardinghouse was home to ten Ascher employees, so it caught the strikers' attention. The home was destroyed; and luckily the tenants were at work at the time of the explosion. Alina's local parish took her in, and the workers were relocated to another company house. Groups of strikers and Citizens' Alliance members watched as firefighters tried to take control of the fire at Alina's. The C & H mounted police had to rush the crowds to disperse them. The horses prancing about seemed to work better than having men break up the crowds on foot. Sheriff Cruse asked for C & H funds to purchase new uniforms for the mounted police. We agreed to purchase new red woolen parkas and trousers for the troops. The riding wave of red should be quite an intimidating sight. Sheriff Cruse expects that the men will be suited up by Friday.

Now that I've broken the ice with Aili again, I couldn't help myself but to go to her today. After her studies were complete with the children, we dressed for the occasion and snowshoed through Tamarack Park. The snow still remained on the pine boughs and it looked as if we were in another world. You could only hear our heavy breathing as we walked towards the falls. Here the water had frozen and had formed elaborate icicles and sculptures. We were exhausted by the time we sat at the frozen falls to rest. Aili had packed two pasties in her coat. As we ate the delicious pastry of potatoes and rutabagas, I told Aili that I wanted to make love to her right there in the snow. "You don't want to get frost bit do you?" she said in jest. "It would be worth it!" I said exasperated. We finished our lunch and made it back to Clara's before dark. Since we were soaked in sweat, Clara thought it would be wise to take a sauna before we became too chilled. We took turns taking a sauna. As I exited to the sub-zero outside, dressed only in a towel, Aili was waiting for me and holding some thin birch saplings. After she made me roll in the snow, she beat my hide with the saplings. I'm not sure if what Aili did to me was tradition, but somehow, as painful as it was, I enjoyed it.

There appears to be desertion among the ranks of the federation members both in Keweenaw and Houghton Counties. Apparently a group of Finns and Hungarians quit the union because their demands for cash payment from the union went unmet. There is also dissatisfaction among the Finns running the Finnish cooperatives because their strike benefits can only be used at the cost stores, where they see prices almost doubled at times. Many strikers have announced their intention of going back to work. Even with such dissension, noisy demonstrations continue throughout the range. In Ricedale, a rail station some 13 miles south of Houghton, the Northern Michigan Special of Chicago, Milwaukee and St. Paul was fired upon. As the train passed a crowd of strikers, the engineer saw a man waving a flag on a stick. Ignoring the possibility of danger, the engineer sent the train on through, where it was immediately fired on. Once the men were safely detrained at Painesdale, the guards went on a search for the gunman. Nothing has yet resulted from the search.

Although most mines are between half and full capacity, the strike condition is just as volatile today as it was on July 23rd. Since only two full troops of guardsmen remain, Sheriff Cruse requested that we meet with the board of supervisors to allow him to organize a stronger force of mounted men. "A force of mounted men will do more than three times the number of foot men in preventing disorder," he said. We will call a special meeting of the board on Monday. Attorneys for the union and the mine companies will meet at the Supreme Court in Lansing on Tuesday. A hearing will be held on the mandamus by which the Supreme Court ruled that the injunction against strike violence, issued and revoked by Judge O'Brien, must stand. Frustrated with the whole mess, I went to the pharmacy to pick up tickets for the C & H sponsored band concert being held at the opera house tonight. Knowing that Aili would probably be listening backstage, I thought that I'd ask her to sit with me in our box seats. I found her tending Clara's bar. She said that she would be flattered to accompany me. When I picked her up at 7 p.m., she looked radiant. Clara had done her hair in a French twist, and she wore a beautiful dress of gold brocade. She was beauty defined.

I was proud to have Aili by my side at the concert. The band was not like the Boston Symphony, which C & H profits helped to unite, but it wasn't bad for Red Jacket. As I walked Aili home we were accosted by a mob of strikers. Big Annie led the mob, and they called Aili a traitor. They even tore at her dress and threw buckets of excrement toward us as we ran for Clara's. "Look at my dress, Eston!" Aili cried. "It will be all right. I will buy you a hundred more dresses just like it!" I said. "They're right, Eston! I can't have it both ways, and neither can you!" she cried. With that, she ran upstairs to her room. Clara just shook her head in disgust and once again suggested that I leave until conditions improve. Today there was the usual Sunday parades and meetings of strikers. The federation men addressed 1,600 men and women in Laurium. These leaders are not yet prepared to give up their struggle.

At the annual convention of the AFL today, speeches were made and resolutions passed in regard to the Michigan copper strike. The resolutions demand a congressional investigation and call for contributions for the support of the Michigan strikers. The federation is also demanding an investigation as to how C & H obtained title to its copper lands. They're asking for an adjustment and retribution. Father was outraged by the words spoken by the Secretary of Labor. Our attorneys sent a petition to President Wilson declaring the Seattle speech socialistic and in conflict with the property right tenets of the Democratic Party. "Men work naked in 8,000 foot level, without ventilation, breathing their own foul air mixed with the poisonous fumes of the metal they dig?" yelled father. "I've never heard such rubbish..." He never finished his sentence. Father collapsed to the floor. I summoned some guardsmen watching our property to help me carry him to the hospital.

Father has had a heart attack. This would explain how tired and run down he's seemed. He is alert but rather weak. The doctors say that he may have future episodes but that he should be able to come home within the week. After I returned home from the hospital, Sheriff Cruse notified me of a riot that occurred at Quincy. Apparently some 70 shots were fired, injuring three and one probably fatally. Blood covered the snow as the troops had to push some 650 miners down the Quincy Hill to restore order. General Abby has summoned the governor for more support than the remaining 250 guardsmen. Relief, however, is unlikely largely due to the recent cries of the WFM and AFL. As we were speaking, a mob of deputies summoned the sheriff from my doorstep. In Laurium, Joseph Hirsch, a deputy and in the employ of C & H, had his house torched by strikers while he and his family slept on the second floor. Earlier in the day he had been threatened with a note pinned to the front door. The note warned him to quit being a deputy, or he would be given reasons to be sorry. Exhausted by the events today, I will retire early and wait for yet another day in Copperdom.

I visited Father first thing today to tell him the latest news of the strike. He advised me to get with the other mine managers to discuss a more aggressive campaign against the strikers. When I got to the office, there was a note lying on my desk from Aili. She had already heard about Father and wished him well. She had also packed a basket of food, knowing that I had probably foregone eating during all the commotion. She apologized for her recent collapse and wished that the company men would make some concessions soon. As I was thinking of Aili, I received a notice stating that Ahmeek, Mohawk and Wolverine have agreed to bring in imported workers. Although our consolidated mines in Quincy and Hancock have already done so, the Keweenaw, our most volatile mine in the zone, hasn't yet seen trainloads of "rolling stones" delivered. Ahmeek is scheduled to have two trainloads arriving. The first will have over 250 workers while the second will have over 1,000. How can concessions be made when we have plenty of willing workers?

Although the WFM parade members have dwindled to 250 or less, they still remain a force to be dealt with. Today over 70 were arrested for demonstrating in violation of the injunction. As the trains loaded with the imported workers arrived in Mohawk, the demonstrations became unruly. Workingmen were escorted by 100 National Guardsmen to the mine. Big Annie was one of the arrested for using foul language to guardsmen and accosting a scab from behind with her flagpole. The remaining strikers are now seeing that we mean business and that their jobs may become permanently filled if they don't return to work. A rally in Laurium on Saturday should prove to be just as violent. Father was pleased that the injunction was resulting in more arrests. He asked how I was getting along as manager and even asked about Aili. He didn't condemn me for having feelings for her but rather asked me to let the future determine our fate. "Attend to your duties at C & H first. Your personal life will take care of itself," he said.

I finally got over to Clara's to thank her for the basket of food. Aili was not there at first, but she returned from school as Clara was putting down a warm bowl of stew for me. Aili, Clara and I conversed about the strike as we ate. I assured them that I would be considering an eight hour day and that we had even considered it before, but many of the strikers didn't want it because it would be an actual cut in their pay. Aili's wide, innocent eyes seemed to believe me, but she wanted me to give her a date. She pressured me into agreeing to an announcement by the end of next week. She and Clara now thought of me as a hero. They were confident that such news would entice the remaining strikers back to work and the WFM out of the district. We enjoyed the rest of our evening sitting in Clara's parlor. Aili looked beautiful as her cheeks flushed from the warmth of the fire. As if Clara could read my thoughts, she left the room so that Aili and I could be alone. Aili sat before the fire, and I knelt down beside her. As we watched the flames and held each other, I breathed in her scent and nuzzled her neck. "It won't be long, my Aili. We will be together soon," I promised. As we remained close, a large explosion startled us.

I ran from Aili's toward the smoke which penetrated the cold winter air. As I ran towards the No. 1 and No. 2 shafts, the snow continued to build in my boots and break my run. By the time I had arrived, the fire wagons were in sight and Sheriff Cruse and a band of armed deputies were standing about a gaping hole at the entrance to the No. 1 shaft. The smell of burning support beams made us gag. Luckily no one was injured during the blast. However, the damage was immense. The mine engineer's office windows shattered with the force of the explosion. Finding the culprits will be difficult. General Abby once again telegraphed the governor about the explosion. He will be in favor of more aggressive tactics to break the strike. At the hospital Father chuckled at the news of the explosion. "Desperate measures for desperate times," he said. "It will end soon, Eston. They have nothing to show for five months of parading but anger. Don't do a thing in regard to concessions."

At the rally in Laurium yesterday foreign speakers who addressed the meeting had the nerve to tell the strikers that their mines now are owned virtually by the government, and before long the government will be operating them. The strikers will then go back to work as government employees. They urged the strikers to stick to the strike until this consummation is brought about. The parade that followed was peaceful, and no arrests were made. I helped Father get checked out of the hospital. It was nice having him home again. I hired a Finnish widow, desperate for work, to make meals and to clean the house. Helmie is a large woman and is as quiet as a church mouse. Father teased me that I could have found someone more appealing to the eye to fuss after him. He told me how the mine lands were acquired years ago and how the federation seems to think that it was all done illegally. "I've already called some representatives in Washington. They will get nowhere with their accusations. The lands are ours and will remain ours," he said breathlessly. With that, he slumbered until dinner.

Another attempt to dynamite a mine compressor and stack occurred last night at the Mohawk mine. Luckily a deputy noticed the sticks before anyone could light the fuses. A search around the mine property turned up no guilty party. Today I discussed with Father my thoughts on offering the employees an eight-hour workday as a partial concession. With the recent attempts against mine property and with the large number of miners returning to work, I thought that this concession just might end the strike for good. Father was against the notion, but he was still too ill to put up a huge fight. "You will have to answer to the owners in Boston if it doesn't work," he said. "I will leave the decision to you, but you must remember that your shareholders come first. How will your decision affect profits? The lode is decreasing as well as the price per ton. Are you jeopardizing the future of C & H by giving in?"

Today the company announced its concessions. Effective December 1st the miners are to get an eight-hour day for underground and a nine-hour day for surface workers. An extra $1 per day will be paid to any miner who works Saturday nights. The company has also promised to pay more attention to the workers' on-the-job needs. Further, we agreed to meet one day each week to hear grievances. There was a large group outside union headquarters. As I passed, I could hear a leader discourage the strikers from taking the concessions. "Hold out for union recognition. They're just giving you a carrot to entice you back to work. Things will remain as they were," he shouted. Father was right. They are ungrateful. I met Aili at the pub for lunch. She was very pleased that I upheld my promise to make concessions. She asked if she and Clara could come to the house to make Thanksgiving dinner for Father and me. Knowing what Father's reaction would be, I discouraged her and blamed it on his health. Since Helmi can take care of Father, I agreed to come to Clara's for the feast. Father had heard about the concessions that I announced. I did not tell him what I had heard outside union headquarters. Surely things will settle down over the upcoming holiday.

Unfortunately my announcement coincided with Judge O'Brien handing out punishment for past strike disorders. Charged back in August, Vasil Kneezovich and Joseph Staduhar were sentenced to 20 days in jail, a large fine and court costs. He also stated the judgment that the police officer didn't handle the arrest properly, but that it didn't give them the right to become unlawful citizens. This news didn't settle well with the remaining strikers. The leaders used it as further ammunition to show how the companies are further punishing the strikers for fighting for their rights. In addition to more fueled parades than usual, I also had non-striking surface men at my office to discuss the dictatorial nature of some of the mine engineers. What have I done? To make matters worse, the Citizens' Alliance, with our dollars used to finance printing costs, published their first issue of *Truth*. The alliance now including Houghton County, has over 5,000 members. *Truth* had applications printed right in it so anyone could join by mailing or delivering it to any member's home or office.

After I had dinner with Father, I left for Clara's. Father was under the assumption that I was going to the office to work. Clara's house was filled with creatures of all nationalities. Women, men, widows and children were served a wonderful meal of turkey and potatoes. Everyone knew who I was, but still they treated me with respect. They thanked me for my recent concessions and assured me that more miners wanted things the way they were than how they are now. Aili talked excitedly about the Mother Goose play that was being planned for the auxillary Christmas party. Only union children are invited. The federation is paying for part of the costs, and they plan to solicit from businesses for the rest of the donations. She said that the federation has already given the cause $63. "Every child will get candy and a gift!" she said. Her face lit up as she discussed the children. I asked, "Aili, what will you do if the strike is over and there is no union presence in Red Jacket?" "Union or no union, we're family now. The children will get their party!" she said.

There still remain over 7,000 strikers in the region. Nonetheless, the zone was quiet today. Perhaps they're contemplating their return to work, or it may be that it's just too cold to parade today. Aili's involvement with the Christmas party has me somewhat bothered. She was never really a member of the federation, but the federation is giving the party for members and their children. I know that Aili means well, but she's not looking at the big picture. She is, in fact, a representative of the union. The union is what this whole strike is about. It's not about the money or work hours. I must talk to her about her involvement. Father's condition hasn't seemed to improve much. I have to stop at the pharmacy to pick up more medicine as prescribed by his doctor. His interest in the strike seems to be dwindling. He's sure that by next week things will be back to normal. I hope that he's right. After listening to Aili and some of the strike leaders, I have my doubts. I haven't heard of any rallies being held here or at the Palestra this weekend. Finally I'll have a weekend just to relax.

I coerced Aili and Clara to go skating last night. Clara was a sight to see on skates. She laughed the whole time that she was up, which wasn't very long, and we laughed right along with her. Afterward, we had tea and cardamom cakes at Clara's. After we had warmed up, we went back outside for a carriage ride. We snuggled under the blankets and enjoyed the fresh, pure air. When I thought the time was right, I brought up Aili's involvement with the union. She assured me that she wasn't a member and that she's just trying to support the children. I explained our perspective and the views of the newly formed Citizens' Alliance group. "I don't care what your groups want. I just know what the children need. I also know about death and fairness. Just because the WFM goes away, this doesn't mean that the workers won't reunite under another name. Your ways provided for our community beautifully. Don't assume my ignorance when it comes to profits being shared lavishly with the shareholders, most of whom don't even live here. The workers want some of that back in the form of safety and quality time with their families. This will never change!" she charged.

Aili and I were quiet during the rest of our carriage drive. She let me walk her to the door, but I didn't get my usual good night kiss. Her words haunt me. She's right in that worker-employer relations will never be the same. This strike has brought employee-employer relations to the media forefront. Not only are our conditions of employment now public across America, but also other company's practices have found their way to the ears of our workers. Working in a copper mine in the Upper Peninsula of Michigan is no longer the only option for families. Already many immigrants have left for Butte, Detroit and Bisbee. Many immigrants have declared their citizenship just so that they can vote in elections. Now hiring the best candidate to fight for their causes is of utmost importance. I'm eager to see just what the results of our concessions will be. Although the weather is cold and blustery today, a few strikers still paraded down the streets. Most were, however, inside the taverns of Red Jacket preparing for a hangover on Monday. Since the mines are closed on Sunday, imbibing is a usual Sunday pastime.

Today I worked analyzing the various pay schedules for all of the positions at the mine. It will be virtually impossible to set a pay scale that is uniform for all of our workers. The other mine managers are in agreement with my assessment. It will also be impossible to eliminate the one-man drill. The present price of copper and our ever decreasing copper content per ton will not allow us to vary from the use of the drill. I was surprised at how few workers actually returned to work after my announcement of concessions. Father tried not to say, "I told you so," but his tone said it for him. "God damn it, Eston. You must make no more concessions. The winter is here. We have replacement workers. Nothing needs to change." His rage caused him to collapse. I could not revive him. Once again I summoned some guards to help me to deliver him to the hospital. This time the doctors were dismal. Aside from strong dose of morphine, there was nothing more that they could do for him. They don't expect his heart to last much longer. He could pass on any day. Dazed, I left the hospital and headed back to my office. I cannot tolerate this strike one day longer. It has nearly eliminated everyone that I love.

Today I announced that if workers don't return by December 19th they will be permanently replaced by imported men. I also announced that all concessions that will be made have been made and that the current pay scales and the use of the one-man drill are here to stay. The Citizens' Alliance members helped to post the announcements at all taverns, co-ops and churches. Immediately the strikers paraded to show their fury. The local strike leaders wired Charles Moyer to notify him of the announcement. Aili arrived at my office by mid-afternoon. She was furious with me for shutting down negotiations. I lost my temper with Aili for the first time. I told her that the strike has nearly killed off my entire family and that I will not tolerate the conditions for one more minute. With tears welling in her eyes she said, "May God save your soul." She stormed out of my office and probably my life forever. I had to have guards escort me across the street to the hospital. I sat with Father until he fell asleep. He was proud of me for finally taking a stance. He was so drugged from the morphine that I could barely understand him as he said, "You've done the right thing, Son."

Judge O'Brien gave the strikers new fuel today as he announced that he was suspending the sentences for the 139 he had found guilty of contempt of court. "Strikers, through enthusiasm for their cause rather than with any intention of deliberately violating the order of the court…were engaged in a heroic struggle for the mere right to retain their membership in a labor organization." He went on to say, "…that the companies had done nothing to conciliate strikers, while doing everything to increase their bitterness and hostility." Judge O'Brien's legal realism, the idea that human experience called for new interpretations of law, infuriated the local establishments. Judge O'Brien has obviously regressed to his days as a labor attorney. In response to the ruling, the Citizens' Alliance members held a meeting at their new headquarters at the Douglass House in Houghton. In the second issue of *Truth*, the alliance detailed how Moyer and other federal agitators are paid to lie, destroy property and assassinate their enemies. In fewer than ten days the alliance has grown to over 9,000 members.

At the meeting of the Citizens' Alliance yesterday it was agreed that the stratum of editors, doctors, barbers, butchers, bankers, lawyers, clergy, Teamsters, shopkeepers and homemakers would back the companies in whatever tactics were necessary to end the strike and rid the zone of the federation. Fearing no one, I made the decision to cut off water and electric from all company owned homes. Though evictions have not occurred, announcements went out restating evictions will occur after the 19th. The strikers rallied once again and resorted to kerosene. The public bathhouse was shut down to prevent the strikers from bathing there instead of their homes. I don't even want to guess Aili's thoughts right now. I fear losing her over this, but the strike must end no matter the cost. While I was at the club, Sheriff Cruse came to my table looking somber. He told me that Father was very ill and that I was to go to the hospital immediately. When I arrived, Father was very pale and barely able to speak. In a state of delirium he said his last words to me. As he shut his eyes for the last time, he said, "Forgive me, Eston. Go to Aili."

I did not go to the office today. I planned Father's funeral for Saturday. A memorial service will be held here and in Boston. I had visitors at the house for the viewing. I was numb with anger and grief. I could not forget his last words. What did he mean by asking for forgiveness? Why would he tell me to go to Aili after he'd put up such a fight against it? Aili arrived with tears streaming down her face. She hugged me and cried for both of us. I was as lifeless as Father. Sensing my state, Aili led me to the parlor sofa. I didn't tell her Father's last words because the strike was still an issue between us. The strike will cease, but the grievances will never end. No matter what I do as a company man, it will be wrong in Aili's eyes. My benevolence is unimportant. What's important to her is how the miners can protect themselves. Aili left, promising to check on me after the funeral tomorrow.

The turnout for Father's funeral was touching. Thousands of people were at the coliseum. Not only were large numbers of alliance members there but also many miners. The few remaining strikers were outside the arena protesting the wrongs they feel that Father had brought against them. I couldn't even escort Father's casket to the cemetery without having guards to push back the strikers. Shortly after I returned home, Aili knocked at the door. I didn't answer it. I needed to be alone. I had to decide which way to go. Should I remain at C & H? Should I go back to Boston? Should I marry Aili? My body is finally shutting down from the stress and I'm retiring early, not knowing what tomorrow will bring.

At two o'clock in the morning a volley of rifle shots crashed into Thomas Dally's house in Painesdale, killing three and wounding a 13-year-old girl. The assailants could not be found, but the WFM ruffians fell under suspicion. I awoke to the rapping on my door by Sheriff Cruse and General Abby. "They have sealed their own doom," said the sheriff. Thousands of alliance members boarded special Copper Range Railroad trains to rally at the Calumet armory. The citizens set into motion a plan to rid the outside agitators from Keweenaw and Houghton County. They are now armed. A virtual civil war has erupted. Those businessmen hesitant to join the alliance have now joined. The region was a tinderbox ready to explode. Our corporate attorneys have warned the alliance members to be lawful while trying to rid the WFM members from the region. The mines and shops will be shut down for a half-day so that those who wish to may attend the funerals of those recently slain.

The strikers, not fearing the alliance members, were out on the street first thing this morning. In the dark they sang Christmas carols at the mine entrances. Final rites for the slain miners were followed by mass rallies at Calumet and Houghton. Some 40,000 marched in Calumet, and over 4,000 crowded into the armory, while 8,000 pushed into the newly opened sports exhibition at the coliseum. Prominent figures spoke of the peace they had known before the WFM. Reverend J.R. Rankin, pastor of Houghton's Grace Methodist Episcopal Church, cried, "What had the WFM cared for laboring men?" The audience shouted back, "Nothing, Nothing!" In response to the Painesdale murders, the media returned. They had originally come to the region to check out the WFM's claims, but were quick to return home because they saw a model community where workers had it better off than most miners across the country. Scuffles broke out throughout the day between the alliance members and the miners. The remaining guardsmen, about 70, were sent to the zone to handle the situation as best as they could. At this point I merely have to sit back and wait for the winner to appear. Charles Moyer returned to the district today. Nobody had seen him since October.

December 12, 1913

The alliance members arranged for raids to occur throughout the region today. Armed alliance members, and deputies without warrants, raided WFM homes and places of business. Raids occurred at Quincy, South Range and even the WFM store on Pine Street. Rifles, revolvers, swords and even dynamite were confiscated. Paddy Dunnigan of Ahmeek exclaimed, "We have 300 rifles right here, and I will be goddamned if any of the officers of Houghton and Keweenaw County can get them away without bloodshed. They will not take them from us just to give them to alliance members so that they can shoot the shit out of us." His cries didn't deter Ahmeek from getting raided. Since only five Waddell and 70 Ascher men remain in the region, Sheriff Cruse arranged for the fire whistles to be blown to summon aid in case of trouble. This way, any armed alliance member or deputy could unite to fight off the strikers. Charles Moyer continued to believe that the cause of the workers could be salvaged. He led his remaining followers to believe that both the state and federal governments were arbitrating the strike. Since Father's death, I have spoken to no one except alliance leaders and Sheriff Cruse.

Our law firm, Rees, Robinson & Peterman, orchestrated rallies today at the Amphidrome in Houghton, the armory in Calumet and the coliseum in Laurium. We hired bands and made special arrangements for trains to deliver workers to the rally free of charge. They were all given the afternoon off so that they could participate. Leaders cried that the "poisonous slime" must be removed. The even ridiculed Judge O'Brien's lenient rulings. The Christmas music at the rally did nothing to get me into a Christmas mood. I've made the decision to leave the region for a short time. I booked passage by rail to Boston. A memorial is scheduled for Father. It will be nice to see family again. I won't tell Aili of my intended departure tomorrow. I discharged Helmi from her duties until after the holiday.

My train departed at 9 o'clock. As my train left the station, I could see the strikers parading the streets of Red Jacket. Luckily I left without anyone noticing. Sheriff Cruse has wiring instructions, should he have to correspond with me. By the time I entered the dinner car, it appeared that I had entered a different world. The snow-covered streets disappeared, and the sky brightened. My mood brightened with each cognac. I secretly toasted to Mother and Father, and tears welled in my eyes as I thought about them. Never did I think that they would have to sacrifice so much for C & H.

My relatives were happy to greet me at the Boston station. The Christmas lights and decorated storefronts brightened my mood. I spent some of my newly acquired inheritance on new suits, shirts and ties. I could shop every day for years before I'd put a dent into my savings. At Mother's favorite jewelry store I even bought a diamond ring for Aili. It was a frivolous act. Father's memorial provided closure for me. In great Boston fashion everyone, including myself, got very drunk at the wake that followed the service. It was nice being home again. My cousins and I had a great time talking about their college experiences. I stayed the night at my parents' brownstone. I will have to hire a team to rid the brownstone of all the articles not wanted. I packed personal items, important to me, away in a cedar chest. Much will be given to charity. The local paper reported that the union in Red Jacket failed to provide the strikers with the promised food and clothing. It was reported that the streets of Red Jacket were quiet and that many were preparing to return to work or leave the region altogether. I'm amazed that the strike has reached national proportions. I will return back to the zone tomorrow. I must finish what's been started.

December 16, 1913

My arrival in Red Jacket won't come quick enough. Today, still on the rail, I was handed a newspaper that had the latest news of the strike. The Supreme Court has issued a permanent injunction against the strikers prohibiting all demonstrations. Further, a Grand Jury investigation into the latest disorders has been planned. All signs would indicate that the strikers are losing steam.

December 17, 1913

When I arrived at the Mineral Range depot, angry strikers who had heard about my scheduled arrival greeted me. When I finally made it home, Sheriff Cruse arrived to brief me on the happenings while I had been gone. He told me that the violence was so frequent that the fire whistles were going off all the time. The hospital was no longer accepting admissions from strikers or their families because the hospital was overcome with strike related injuries. Only the Citizens' Alliance members would be helped if needed. I went to Clara's to see if Aili was available. She was at the Italian Hall preparing for the Christmas party and play. The Italian Benefit Society leases the first floor of the hall to a bar and the Great Atlantic & Pacific Tea Company. I climbed the stairs to the second floor hall and found Aili covered in down feathers, the result of her making the goose outfit for the play. She was excited to see me and asked if I was feeling better. I told her about my trip and asked if she would spend Christmas Day with me. She agreed to see me on Christmas Day. My proposal of marriage will be a complete surprise.

My first day back to the office was no less stressful than prior to my trip to Boston. Several shop owners and the president of Red Jacket village came to see me to request that I extend the reinstatement period for the strikers to January 1st. I agreed that I would and that I'd get the other operators to comply. The community leaders spent many hours today trying to convince the strikers to return to work. Few responded to their pleas. Moyer has asked Judge O'Brien to impose an injunction against the Citizens' Alliance due to their frequent violent acts against the strikers. He's considering their request. The Houghton Trades and Labor Council wired Governor Ferris and asked for a federal investigation into the affairs of the alliance. Ferris had me document our recent concessions as well as the reasons for not conceding to the other strike issues. In response to the request for a federal investigation, several business owners wired the governor denouncing the idea. Governor Ferris has also wired President Wilson deploring the idea as well. Law and order have prevailed since December 10th, and under the united demands of the citizens, we will prevail from now on.

Even with the extended reinstatement in place, the WFM members are doing what they can do to stop the importation of workers. I've heard that they are paying up to $250 and a free train ride home if they'd leave the region. The owners have requested that we take a tough stance. The WFM has weakened enough that production hasn't even been affected. Governor Ferris has sent Grant Fellows, Michigan's Attorney General, to examine the situation. He will find that the district has become as quiet as a country churchyard. Since Sheriff Cruse has prohibited the use of all public halls, Fellows won't even be able to see the union members at an organized meeting. I stopped by Clara's this evening for supper. After a plate of beefsteak pie and dessert of saffron cake, Aili and I talked of her plans for the Christmas party. Because money is low, the tree will only be decorated with pink and blue crepe paper and ten cents worth of tinsel. The Mother Goose play, a ballerina and traditional Christmas carols will provide the necessary entertainment. Gifts for the children will include handmade stockings and mittens and chocolate drops. Even though the party is union related, I find myself just as excited about it as Aili. We are both eager to see what the New Year will bring to us.

Campaigns still rage on both sides. The various businessmen are pleading to the strikers in several languages to return to work before January 1st. J.P. Peterman of Mohawk has even offered that if the strikers return, he will give in to their demands prior to the first payday. The federation called this a "sop" to trick the strikers back to work. To hold them off longer, the federation came up with $7 for each member. With the strike at an apparent standstill, I had few interruptions at the office. How did Father do this job for so long? The weekend is before me, and I have made no plans. Aili will be at the opera house raiding the wardrobe room for costumes for the Mother Goose play. Since things seem to be running smoothly for the time being, I'd better leave her be. She's too preoccupied with the party to think about anything else.

Mor Oppman, the lead agitator of the WFM, was arrested today after the sheriff raided his home. Four sticks of dynamite and a considerable fuse were found in his home. His bond was set for $2,000! With the lead socialist incarcerated, the striking numbers are dismal. There are even rumors that the miners of Copper City, Houghton, Hancock and Portage Lake plan on returning to work. The Michigan Federation board members arrived at the district today. It's uncertain whether or not a rally will be held tomorrow. With Christmas nearing and with many considering the return to work, it's unlikely that they would have much of a crowd anyway. Moyer is nothing but a walking delegate and agitator, trying to stir up as much trouble as necessary to profit financially to hold on to his position. If he pulls out now, it's likely that his entire operation will be shattered nationwide. In the spirit of Christmas, I went to our attic this evening to find Mother's Christmas decorations. I put out a few, and then I went to the club to have drinks with Sheriff Cruse. He notified me that General Abby and the remaining troops will leave tomorrow.

The Michigan Federation of Labor Board announced that it would call a general labor convention within the next 30 days to consider resolutions to the strike. Many of Red Jacket's community members feel that this is too much, too late. Besides, any resolutions derived from such a meeting would surely benefit the strikers, not the company owners. It's been estimated that this strike has cost some $6 million so far, split between the companies, state and union donations. Clearly the federation is trying to convince Moyer to reconsider the union demands. The streets were quiet after the board members left the depot. The strikers that remain quickly left for home, possibly to consider what was said and whether or not it would dissuade them from returning to work. I went to the Italian Hall to see if Aili was available for dinner. She declined because she was busy opening several barrels of chocolate candies. Walking home, I passed several people asking for donations for the needy. I fed one kettle so much money that I'm sure it will buy food baskets for hundreds. The woman asking for the donation was shocked. She didn't know who I was, for which I was thankful.

Today I found Aili at the Lutheran church filling baskets for the needy. The baskets contained roast beef, butter, bread, apples, corn, coffee, nuts and cake. Aili was flushed with excitement when she told me about the mysterious donor. "Miracles do exist!" she cried. "Oh, Eston, everything seems to be getting back to normal." She begged me to recognize the union. "They won't ask any more of you. They just want the power to unite if they feel there's a worthy cause. You have to admit their demands have been warranted. Please, Eston, please! End the strike!" I could not believe what I was hearing. My face must have given away my thoughts because Aili burst into laughter. She laughed as she said, "All right, All right! It can wait until after the holiday!" Still flustered and speechless, I walked Aili down Fifth Street. The merchants were putting up their Christmas displays, despite having very few shoppers.

Judge O'Brien ruled in favor of an injunction to restrain the Citizens' Alliance members from doing acts of violence to federation officials and agitators. The Citizens' Alliance members are furious with the ruling. Immediately Sheriff Cruse was called to break up disorders between the two groups. Sheriff Cruse had to enforce the ruling, although he was biased and opted to turn the cheek on many blatant violations. It was poor judgment for the judge to announce such a ruling so close to Christmas. What seemed to be a dying ember now has burst into a hotbed of fury.

The Opera House and Red Jacket Town Hall.

Tragedy struck Red Jacket yesterday. Apparently at about 4:30 panic set in at the Italian Hall. A cry of "Fire!" in two different languages caused a mad rush to the stairwell of the hall. As mostly women and children tried to exit the long and narrow stairwell, the panic caused several to fall against the doors, which open inward. Many were piled on top of each other and were crushed to death. In the end, seventy-four women, men and children died for a claim of fire that never existed. Witnesses claim that a man wearing an alliance button yelled "Fire!" The Red Jacket firehouse had received notice early on, but felt that it was just another scuffle between the strikers and alliance members. By the time they had arrived, the dead bodies were stacked four to five thick. The firemen had to remove the bodies from the second floor and work their way down since it was impossible to open the doors to the hall. I ran to the hall as soon as I heard about the tragedy. I used the fire escape to enter the building. I retched as I saw Aili's body, unconscious, and pressed against the wall to the stairway. In her raised arms she firmly grasped a child of less than one year old. The infant was still alive.

The 74 bodies were taken to the Red Jacket town hall. Tables were strewn with bodies, mostly dead children. Several of those thought to be dead were revived at the tavern below the hall. Help poured in from all over the country today. In conjunction with the Citizens' Alliance, we offered $25,000 to the victims' families. Moyer announced, "The Western Federation of Miners will bury its own dead…the American labor movement will take care of the relatives of the deceased. No aid will be accepted from any of these citizens who a short time ago denounced these people as undesirable citizens." I was abhorred that Moyer would use such a tragedy to benefit his cause. A special memorial meeting was called at the opera house. A committee of twelve, each nationality being fairly represented, was put together to make arrangements for the funerals and to offer assistance to the families of the victims. I ordered all of the hospitals to be opened to the injured. Every physician, ambulance, automobile and undertaker was called upon to help with the rescue and burial. In a statement made to the United Press, Moyer declared that the Citizens' Alliance was at fault for the tragedy.

Special trains arrived today with pine caskets. The image of the caskets lined down Fifth Street will never leave my mind. Moyer, after dining with Charles Tanner, the unions traveling auditor, was approached by Sheriff Cruse and Attorney Peterman. They asked that Moyer retract his statement blaming the Citizens' Alliance. Initially he refused but then said that he would try to discourage the circulation of rumors. Shortly after Sheriff Cruse left, it's reported that Moyer was ambushed by what's believed to be Citizens' Alliance members. In a scuffle Moyer was shot in the spine. He and Tanner were dragged from the Scott Hotel to the Copper Range depot in Houghton. Here the men were put on trains to Chicago, and shouts of "If you ever come back here again, we'll hang you!" rose above the sound of the train's locomotives.

Moyer arrived in Chicago today. From his hospital bed he told of his attack and continued to denounce the mine owners as thugs. He told an AP reporter, "I believe the strike is won!" Oblivious to the suffering going on in Red Jacket, Moyer continued to fight for his cause. Over 20,000 people gathered to attend the funeral of the dead. The townspeople followed the pine caskets for adults and the white caskets for children. The five-mile procession and funerals didn't end until after 6 o'clock. Two mass graves were dug. One was for the Protestants, the other for the Catholics. Nummivuori and three other employees of *The Tyomies* were arrested for printing maliciously false articles regarding the Italian Hall tragedy. A jury has called in more than 69 people to hear their versions of the "Italian Hall Disaster".

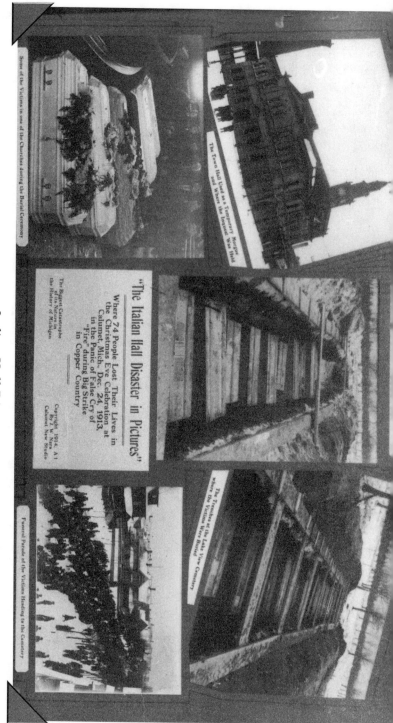

~ Italian Hall Disaster: ~

Some of the Victims in one of the Churches during the Burial Ceremony

The Town Hall Used as a Temporary Morgue and Where the Inquest Was Held

"The Italian Hall Disaster in Pictures"

Where 74 People Lost Their Lives, in
the Christmas Eve Celebration at
Calumet, Mich., Dec. 24, 1913,
in the Panic of False Cry of
"Fire" during Big Strike
in Copper Country

The Biggest Catastrophe
of Its Nature in
the History of Michigan

Copyright 1914, A 1
By J. W. Nara
Calumet New Studio

The Trenches at the Lake View Cemetery
where the Victims Were Buried

Funeral Parade of the Victims Heading to the Cemetery

Interior in the Hall as it Appeared the Next Morning

The Italian Hall in Mourning, the Next Day After Disaster

Interior of the Kitchen as it Looked the Next Morning

101

December 24, 1959

Finally Eston answers the phone. He grimaces as he listens to the trial judge tell him that a decision has been made in favor of his client. Eston's perfect record as a labor attorney will remain intact. The door to his study opens just as he hangs up the phone. The sound of Christmas carols playing and the smell of Aili's freshly baked cardamom braid bring Eston forward to the Christmas of today. Gleefully, Aili says, "Eston! Hurry and put on your Santa suit! The kids will be here shortly!" As he sits holding the red suit, he's ever mindful of the Red Jacket that changed his and others lives, the one that is now just a ghost blanketing our actions of tomorrow.

~

C & H never did fully give up paternalism to recognize labor unions. Many strikes have occurred since the great one of 1913, but one final series of negotiations during 1969 closed the C & H mine forever.

~ *All that remains of the Italian Hall* ~

Bibliography

Biesanz, Mavis H. Helmi Mavis: A Finnish American Girlhood. Waite Park, Minnesota: Park Press, Inc., 1989.

Eiola, Patricia J. A Finntown of the Heart. St. Cloud, Minnesota: North Star Press of St. Cloud, Inc., 1998.

Friggens, Thomas G. No Tears in Heaven. Lansing, Michigan: Michigan Historical Center, Michigan Department of State, 1988.

Germain P. Lest We Forget. Calumet Michigan: P. Germain, 1987.

Lankton, Larry. Cradle to Grave. New York, New York: Oxford University Press, Inc., 1991.

Mason, Philip P. Copper Country Journal: The Diary of Schoolmaster Henry Hobart, 1863-1864. Detroit: Wayne State University Press, 1991.

Monette, Clarence J. The Calumet Theatre. Lake Linden, Michigan: Clarence J. Monette, 1979.

Reeves, Pamela. Ellis Island. Barnes & Noble, Inc., 1998.

Simonson, Dorothy. The Diary of an Isle Royale School Teacher. Hancock, Michigan: Book Concern Printer, 1996.

Stanley, Jerry. Big Annie of Calumet. New York, New York: Crown Publishers, 1996.

Thomas, Newton G. The Long Winter Ends. Detroit, Michigan: Wayne State University Press, 1941.

Thurner, Arthur W. Calumet Copper and People. Hancock, Michigan: Privately Published, Book Concern Printers, 1974.

Thurner, Arthur W. Rebels on the Range. Lake Linden, Michigan: John H. Forster Press, 1984.

Thurner, Arthur W. Strangers and Sojourners. Detroit, Michigan: Wayne Stat University Press, 1994.

The Daily Mining Gazette, Houghton, Michigan, 1913.

The Marquette Mining Journal, Marquette, Michigan, 1913.